Jacob turned and saw a man wrap one hand around Brie's mouth and the other around her waist.

"Let her go," Jacob demanded, launching himself off the porch.

He was grabbed from behind by a big guy who applied a headlock, restricting Jacob's movement.

Something pinched Jacob's neck, and he was shoved to the ground. As he tried to get up, the guy kicked him in the gut.

He could hear Brie's muffled cries against her attacker's palm.

"You'll keep quiet?"

She nodded, and he removed his hand. "Don't hurt him. Please, don't hurt him."

Jacob coughed and tried to stand again, but something slammed against his back, pinning him in place.

"Stay down," a deep voice ordered.

"I'll go with you," Brianna said. "Leave him here and I'll go without protest."

"No can do. He's coming

And the world faded int

An eternal optimist, **Hope White** was born and raised in the Midwest. She and her college sweetheart have been married for thirty years and are blessed with two wonderful sons, two feisty cats and a bossy border collie. When not dreaming up inspirational tales, Hope enjoys hiking, sipping tea with friends and going to the movies. She loves to hear from readers, who can contact her at hopewhiteauthor@gmail.com.

Books by Hope White

Love Inspired Suspense

Hidden in Shadows
Witness on the Run
Christmas Haven
Small Town Protector
Safe Harbor
Baby on the Run
Nanny Witness
Mountain Hostage

Boulder Creek Ranch

Wilderness Hideout

Echo Mountain

Mountain Rescue
Covert Christmas
Payback
Christmas Undercover
Witness Pursuit
Mountain Ambush

Visit the Author Profile page at LoveInspired.com.

WILDERNESS HIDEOUT

HOPE WHITE

LOVE INSPIRED SUSPENSE
INSPIRATIONAL ROMANCE

LOVE INSPIRED® SUSPENSE
INSPIRATIONAL ROMANCE

ISBN-13: 978-1-335-72283-6

Wilderness Hideout

Copyright © 2021 by Pat White

Recycling programs
for this product may
not exist in your area.

This edition published by arrangement with Harlequin Books S.A.

For questions and comments about the quality of this book, please contact us at CustomerService@Harlequin.com.

Love Inspired
22 Adelaide St. West, 40th Floor
Toronto, Ontario M5H 4E3, Canada
www.LoveInspired.com

Printed in U.S.A.

As every man hath received the gift,
even so minister the same one to another,
as good stewards of the manifold grace of God.
—1 Peter 4:10

This book is dedicated to compassionate friends who listen with an open heart and don't judge, but simply have the courage to hold space.

ONE

Run, girl, run!

Brianna gasped and sat straight up.

Fighting the throbbing pain of a headache, she struggled to remember where she was. Tall coniferous trees surrounded her, the sound of rushing water echoed through the forest and clumps of snow dotted the ground.

She realized her jeans were damp and her hands muddy.

What was she doing out here? Panic rose in her chest. She shook it off. Fear would block her ability to process the situation. Cautiously standing, she hissed against a sharp pain shooting up her leg. She'd injured her ankle. She sat back down and reached into her pocket for her cell phone.

No phone. The only thing in her pocket was a tin of tummy-soothing lozenges. She wasn't wearing her cross-body bag, either.

"She's down there!" a male voice shouted from above.

"Get her!" another responded.

Heart racing, she stood and clenched her teeth against the pain shooting up her leg. She had to get away, had to find help.

Desperately scanning the forest, she spotted a trail leading deeper into the woods. She'd find shelter there, a natural hiding place like a cave, until the danger had passed.

Danger? Why was she in danger?

The panic started again. She used a breathing technique developed for her research study to calm her sympathetic nervous system. In this situation it was normal to be in fight-or-flight mode. But too much adrenaline could impact good decision making.

As she headed toward a trail, she clicked into scientist mode and focused on identifying where the voices were coming from.

"Do you think she survived the fall?"

The man sounded like he was up above on the ridge.

Not man—men. One was speaking to the other, so there were at least two of them, maybe…more?

She was outnumbered both literally and figuratively. She seemed to be suffering from brain trauma, indicated by her throbbing head and inability to remember how she'd ended up in the forest.

Alone.

Being pursued by men with firm, determined voices.

Heading deeper into the woods, she struggled to remember something, anything about her current situation.

Knowledge is power. Her mantra. Yet right now, she felt utterly powerless.

She needed to change that mindset in order to survive.

"The university conference," she said softly.

That's right. She had come to Montana to speak at a university about her current research into natural healing alternatives to drug therapies. Which still didn't answer the question of how she'd ended up out here in the mountains.

"I'm going down!" a voice echoed.

A shudder raced across her shoulders. She grabbed a tree branch off the ground for support in order to walk faster. Hobbling away, she fought the anxiety taunting her thoughts.

Be calm, she coached herself.

Brie was intelligent and resourceful. That resourcefulness had helped her survive a tumultuous, unfortunate childhood. Her belief in herself protected her from crippling words spoken by toxic adults.

She would not give up, would not let her life end in the middle of some random forest. She still had work to do, people to help. People like…

A choked gasp caught in her throat. This level

of emotion was uncharacteristic of Brie. It must be the head injury. They tended to make people feel insecure and frightened, to act out of character. At least she hadn't totally lost her critical thinking skills, which could potentially save her life.

Save her life? Was her life at risk? The answer resonated deep in her chest: *yes*.

Blocking out the physical pain of her injured ankle, she forged ahead, toward the sound of water.

An image flashed across her mind: sitting in a boat with Dad, fishing. Quiet. Peaceful. He'd cast a smile her way that warmed her insides, then he'd say, *You're going to do great things, Brianna.*

A gunshot cracked across the mountainside, and she instinctively ducked.

Someone was shooting at her?

"What are you doing!"

She scrambled beneath a tree's low-hanging branches for cover.

"I was shooting at a bobcat," a man said.

"Well, stop and focus on finding her!"

Pine needles pricked her cheek. Brie knew staying hidden wasn't the best strategy. It was only a matter of time before they tracked her down and…and what? Why did they want to find her? To hurt her?

Blocking out the presence of her pursuers, she

continued toward the rushing water, intent on her goal: *find safety.*

As the anxiety rose against her will, she decided to sing softly to assuage her fear. Singing was a proven technique to calm the nervous system by stimulating the vagus nerve, therefore reducing panic and anxiety.

"Oh, the weather outside is frightful," she began softly, because Christmas lyrics were the only ones she could remember. "But the fire is so delightful."

In the distance, the sound of water continued to calm her racing heart, probably because of the early memories of her father.

"And since we've no place to go, let it snow, let it snow, let it snow."

She pushed through the trees and approached a robust river. Water rushed from the falls on the right and downstream for what seemed like miles. She considered crossing it, but she wasn't the best swimmer. Her time had been better spent in the lab than partaking in recreational activities.

She eyed the depth of the water, considering her options.

"Dr. Wilkes?"

She spun around and automatically aimed the walking stick like a sword. Twenty feet away stood a tall man in his forties wearing a brown parka. He had dark, hooded eyes and an angular chin.

"Dr. Wilkes," he greeted. He was six feet tall, probably two hundred pounds compared to Brie's five foot two, one hundred and twenty.

"What do you want?"

"I'm Stan. I'm here to help."

"Help with what?"

"I'm with security for the university. You need to come with me."

Why would the university send security for her?

"I'd like to see your identification," she said.

He smiled, a wicked twinkle in his dark brown eyes.

"Stay away," she said.

Instead, he took a few steps forward.

She swung the branch, and he grabbed the other end. He was nearly twice her size, broad shouldered, and he was not respecting her wishes.

They both clung to their respective ends of the branch. If he pulled her close enough to grab her...

A slight curl of his lips made her skin crawl.

She released the stick and stepped back on her injured ankle.

It gave way.

She swung her arms.

And fell backward into the water.

* * *

Jacob's weekend retreat had been both invigorating and relaxing—until he'd heard the woman's scream.

Instinct kicked in, and he mounted his horse to head upriver and check it out. He was tempted to call 9-1-1 but wasn't sure what to report yet. It could be someone playing around with friends or family.

Yet Jacob's gut told him it was a different kind of scream—a cry for help.

Then again, he could be misinterpreting the sound due to his background of always being on guard, ready to solve a crisis at any moment.

Something caught his eye across the river.

"Whoa, girl," he said to Star, his Appaloosa.

He pulled out his binoculars, peered across the river and saw a woman tumble into the water. A man stood on the riverbank, but he didn't try to help, didn't even offer a branch or something for her to grasp on to.

The woman flailed her arms as she was pulled by the current. He redirected his attention downriver to assess the best place to intercept her. Another scream echoed through the mountains.

The woman's head bobbed above the water's surface, then disappeared.

He had to move fast if he was going to help her. Jacob made a clicking sound and directed Star south. Because he knew this area pretty well, he was in a good position to track and re-trieve her. He urged Star to pick up her pace.

What a chaotic way to end his retreat, but he'd become an expert at going with the flow and trusting in God's plan for him, even if it seemed random and off course.

As he closed in on the woman's location, he pulled out his phone to call for help. No signal. He shoved the device back into his pocket and focused on getting to her.

Saving her.

There'd been too many he couldn't save as a community crisis officer back in Detroit. Young folks lost to personal demons, misunderstand-ings or abuse.

He gauged the flow of the river to time this just right.

"C'mon, girl," he encouraged Star.

Another scream pierced the crisp afternoon air. Good, the woman was fighting to stay alive. It's when the countryside went quiet that he'd re-ally worry.

Worry that he was too late.

Again.

He pulled Star to a halt and dismounted. Tying her to a tree, he whipped out his binoculars and saw the woman floating toward him. He shucked his coat, shirt and boots, tied a rope around his waist and secured the other end to a tree to make sure the current didn't pull him downriver toward the falls.

Jacob slipped into the water, clenching his teeth against the chill.

At this temperature he figured it wouldn't take long for hypothermia to kick in, which meant the woman would need to be warmed up, and fast.

Struggling against the current, he eyed the best spot from which to grab her. He managed to make his way to a boulder in the middle of the river. Now if he could only reach the blonde woman as she drifted past.

"Help!" she croaked.

"Over here!" he shouted.

She flailed her arms, managing to stay afloat.

"Look out!" he called.

She started to turn and slammed into a boulder.

Her head snapped back.

Her body went limp.

"No," he ground out. He fought the current, fought to get to her before she was sucked down by the falls.

His foot slipped, and he fell below the water's surface; he popped back up in time to grab the woman's leg as she floated past.

The water's chill numbed his hands, but he wouldn't let go.

He pulled her toward him. Inch by inch. Got her close enough to wrap one arm around her torso. Needing both hands to pull them back to shore, he loosened the rope and secured it under her arms. That's when he noticed blood seeping from a wound on her head.

Securing her to his body, he pulled both of them toward land, hand over hand.

She was petite, which made this rescue that much easier.

He couldn't help but wonder what had happened and who the man was on the opposite side of the river. Was he her boyfriend? Had they argued and she'd slipped? Why didn't he at least try to save her? Jacob decided those details were up to authorities to investigate.

Jacob hoped he could get a cell signal when he reached shore, and sooner rather than later. His first aid skills were solid but limited. Depending on her mental state when she regained consciousness, the woman would probably need a CT scan to determine the extent of her head injury. Jacob prayed it wasn't serious.

He'd know soon enough.

His foot touched a rock, then another. The water grew shallow as he approached the riverbank. Now able to stand, he wrapped an arm around the woman's torso and held on to her as he struggled against the weight of their wet clothes. Feet firmly on the ground, he untied her and scooped her up into his arms, making his way back to Star.

He cast a quick glance over his shoulder, wondering if her male friend would come looking for her. There was an old but sturdy bridge about half a mile to the south that locals used, yet those unfamiliar with the area might consider it too dangerous to cross.

Jacob set the woman down, and she groaned, pressing her hand against her head. He grabbed a blanket off his saddle, which he'd packed for his overnight stay in the wilderness. It was the biannual commitment he'd made to himself just over a year ago when he'd started his new life in Montana with a daughter he never knew he had until he'd moved here. His solitary retreats would allow him to commune with God in the beauty of the wilderness. He found peace out here, quieting the nonstop noise of the ridiculousness of life.

As he wrapped the blanket securely around the woman's body, he thought about Cassie, his ex-fiancée and his daughter's mom. His relationship with Cassie had occurred at a time in his life when he didn't take such bonds as seriously as he should have. As he thought of her now, he wondered why no one had helped her on the fateful night of her death. Oh, how he wished he had been there.

But he wasn't.

Shake it off, man. This was not the time to be

distracted by the past. The woman lying before him needed his help.

He dug for the first aid kit in his pack. The head wound would take priority. First, he'd call for help. He pulled his phone out and sighed with relief when he saw he had bars.

"Nine-one-one, what is your emergency?"

"This is Jacob Rush. I pulled a young woman out of Spruce River, about half a mile north of the old Graystone Bridge. She's semiconscious and needs medical assistance."

"West or east side of the river?"

"West."

"What's the young woman's name?"

"I don't know. I don't know her."

"Could...her..."

"Hello?"

"...check the..."

"Hello? Can you hear me?"

Nothing. The call had dropped. He tried again but couldn't get a strong enough signal. Well, he'd given them a location, so at least they knew where to send help.

Jacob grabbed the first aid kit and a ground cloth and turned to the woman.

She was trembling uncontrollably. Not good.

He spread out the cloth to insulate her from the cold earth.

That alone wouldn't stop her from trembling. He quickly slipped off her jacket and wet rain pants, which had kept her jeans dry. Her fleece and long-sleeved shirt were relatively dry thanks to the water-resistant gear. Wrapping her body in the wool blanket, he lowered her onto the padded fabric. Keeping her horizontal was important, as was slow movement. Excessive movement could trigger cardiac arrest.

The additional first aid classes he'd taken shortly before he'd moved to Montana to be with Miri certainly came in handy today. He'd wanted to prepare himself to be the best father possible for the little girl who'd lost her mother at such an early age. After moving to the Boulder Creek Guest Ranch to help raise Miri, with the assistance of Cassie's extended family, he'd continued learning new skills like caring for and riding horses, along with wilderness survival skills. He was surprised at how easily he'd adjusted to his new life as a single dad and rancher.

Which was why he was able to care for the injured woman he'd pulled out of the river, at least until help arrived. Although Emergency knew his location, Jacob didn't expect them for at least half an hour, and that was being optimistic. He decided to start a fire to warm the chill from the woman's body.

The woman. He wished he knew her name. He didn't want to dig through her pockets looking for a wallet. His first priority was making sure she didn't suffer from hypothermia.

He started a fire using wood and kindling he'd brought along for his trip. Once the flame burned steady, he went to the other side of his horse to change into dry clothes. He didn't want to startle her if she regained consciousness and saw a nearly naked stranger standing there.

He dug into his pack for a towel and fresh clothes. As he pulled the clothes out, something fell to the ground. He picked it up—a bright pink piece of paper tied haphazardly around a bag of chocolate candies, courtesy of Miri.

He smiled as he tucked the candy into his pack. To think only a year ago he didn't know he had a daughter.

"No! Help!" the woman cried.

Jacob glanced around the horse.

She was struggling against the blanket. "I can't move!"

"Hang on, you're okay." He went to her side and loosened the blanket.

She edged away from him, her brown eyes flaring with fear.

That's when he realized he was only dressed in his undershirt and jeans.

"Sorry, I was changing into dry clothes," he explained.

She didn't look comforted.

He stepped back and put his hands out in a calming gesture. "I'm Jacob. I pulled you out of the river. I'll be going over there to finish getting dressed."

She sat up and dislodged her arms. Studying her clothes, she said, "My coat? My rain pants?"

"They were soaked, so I removed them. I didn't want you to get hypothermia."

On cue, her body started trembling again, and the blanket slid off her right shoulder. "My body temperature…must be below…ninety-five degrees…"

Not exactly the reaction he'd expected, but okay. He took a tentative step toward her.

"Stay wrapped up, all right?" He put up a hand, and she eyed it suspiciously. He slowly adjusted the blanket so it would cover her shoulder. "The fire will help."

She nodded.

"Like I said, I'm Jacob. And you are?"

"Dr. Wilkes."

Interesting that she didn't share her first name. Whatever work she did as a doctor must be very important to her.

"Nice to meet you, Dr. Wilkes." He didn't offer to shake hands, because he didn't want to frighten her by encroaching on her personal space. "Medical help is on the way. I'm going to get dressed."

He went to the other side of Star and put on his flannel shirt.

"Jacob?"

"Yes," he said, changing into dry jeans and tucking in his flannel shirt.

"I'm confused."

"You have a head injury, so that's normal."

"Not…for me…it isn't."

He put on his jacket and stepped around the horse. Dr. Wilkes had paled and seemed emotionally untethered.

"Hey, could you lie back down for me?" he coaxed, remembering the rule about keeping someone with hypothermia horizontal. Yet she was talking, so that was a good sign, right?

"I shouldn't…be out here," she said, struggling to stand.

"Whoa, there."

She wavered and plopped back down, clinging to the blanket with white-knuckled fingers.

"C'mon, let's wrap you up again and raise your body temperature." When she didn't argue, he pulled the blanket tighter around her shoulders. The scent of mint wafted up to his nostrils.

"Who are you?" she said, studying him with curious brown eyes.

Her intense gaze was disarming.

"You forgot my name already?" he teased. Teasing and joking were his default in awkward situations.

"Jacob," she said.

"That's right. Jacob Rush." He turned to stoke the fire.

"Why…are you here?" she said.

"I heard you scream and saw you fall into the river."

She slowly turned to gaze at the river. "I fell?"

"I think so. I doubt you'd intentionally go for a swim in the Spruce River this time of year."

"Spruce River," she said softly, then eyed the massive trees surrounding them. "But, what am I doing out here?"

"You don't remember?"

She shook her head and nibbled her lower lip.

A similar charactcristic of Miri's when about to have a meltdown.

"It'll come back to you," he said in a comforting tone. "You have a head injury, maybe a concussion, which is contributing to your confusion."

"I don't like that diagnosis."

"Well, I'm no doctor, so it's an educated guess. However, I'd like to offer first aid. You're bleeding." He pointed to his own head.

She touched her head in the samc spot, analyzed her blood-smudged fingers and frowned.

"May I get a closer look?" he said.

She shook her head *no*.

"It might take Emergency a while to get here. We're a solid half hour from town."

"Which town?"

Oh man, this was bad.

"Boulder Creek, Montana."

She seemed to consider that for a minute, as if trying to piece together how she'd ended up out here.

"About your head wound—"

"No, thank you."

He sat across the fire from her and considered strategies to make her more comfortable in order to change her mind. He had to build trust between them. Although Jacob considered himself a kind man, he was, in fact, a complete stranger to Dr. Wilkes.

"I moved out here a year and a half ago from Detroit," he started. "Grew up in the Midwest." He almost asked where she was from but didn't want to risk her not remembering, which could trigger more anxiety.

"So, I was a Midwestern boy until God brought me out West to become a cowboy, sort of."

"God?" she said.

He sensed a note of distaste in her voice.

"Or fate," he said, "Whatever you want to call it. I went from being a social worker with the Detroit PD to being a full-time father of a precocious little girl, and a ranch hand."

"A social worker." She narrowed her eyes at him.

"Yeah, which makes me a good listener," he offered.

She pulled the blanket tighter across her shoulders and gazed into the fire.

Be vulnerable.

"It's strange how life throws you curveballs when you least expect it," he continued.

"Like me ending up in a forest and not remembering how I got here?" She looked up at him. "You saw me fall into the river?"

"Yes, ma'am."

"Wait, you were partially clothed because you jumped into the river to rescue me?"

He nodded affirmative.

"Oh. I... Thank you," she said softly.

"You're welcome."

A few minutes of silence passed. To a passerby, they probably looked like a couple enjoying a peaceful respite in nature. But there was nothing peaceful about the worried frown on Dr. Wilkes's face.

"I wish I remembered what I was doing out here," she said.

"Maybe you were enjoying a relaxing hike?"

She shook her head. "I don't have time for hikes."

"That's a shame."

"My work is too important to be taking frivolous hikes," she snapped, as if he'd challenged the very core of her existence.

He'd gotten rusty in the year he'd not been practicing. "Sorry. I didn't mean to offend you."

She sighed. "No, I apologize for my sharp tone. I'm processing resentment, because if I hadn't been out here doing who knows what, I wouldn't have fallen into the water and injured myself. This isn't like me. I'm usually more sensible, not so—" she hesitated "—weak."

"Maybe your friend can shed some light on the situation."

"Friend?"

"The man you were with?"

The frown deepened, as if she was unable to remember him.

"You'll be okay, Dr. Wilkes."

She glared at him. "You are not a medical doctor and I haven't had a CT scan, so we don't know that I'll be okay, do we?" She shook her head and closed her eyes briefly. "That's not like me. I have better manners than to snap at the man who saved my life."

"No worries. I'd be cranky, too, in your position."

She glanced across the river and shuddered, as if realizing how close she'd come to a more serious, maybe even lethal outcome. But she wasn't trembling from the chill, so that was good.

"I'd be less irritable if I could get back to town."

Her brown eyes had warmed to a deep caramel color, and her cheeks were almost pink. Still, he didn't want to risk irritating her condition by bringing her back on his own.

He gave the fire another poke to encourage

the warmth of new flame. "I'll try calling to get the ETA of the response team."

"Try?"

He stood. "Can't always find a signal out here. Stay bundled up, okay?"

She nodded.

He went to Star and pulled an extra sweatshirt out of his bag. He gently tossed it to her, and she caught it. Good, her reflexes seemed normal.

"It'll be big but will keep you warm."

"Thank you."

He offered a slight smile, turned and headed toward the spot where he'd made the call before. Checked his phone for bars. Nothing. He continued up a trail another hundred feet, then another fifty when finally, the bars appeared in the corner of his screen.

"Got a signal!" he called to Dr. Wilkes.

He wondered what it would take for her to share her first name with him.

"Nine-one-one Emergency," the operator answered.

"It's Jacob Rush. I called earlier about a woman I rescued from the river. Her name is Dr. Wilkes and we're about two miles from the Nickelback Trailhead."

A firm arm wrapped around his neck, pressing on his windpipe and cutting off air. Struggling to free himself, Jacob dropped the phone and pulled against his attacker's arm, but Jacob was at a disadvantage.

Jacob elbowed the guy, and he grunted but didn't let go. Instead, he pulled tighter on Jacob's neck. Stars floated across his vision. No, he couldn't die this way.

Miri. God, I can't abandon Miri.

As he struggled harder, the pressure increased against his neck.

Just relax, a voice said.

He closed his eyes, said a prayer and watched the surrounding trees blur into a mass of green.

TWO

As Brie stared into the fire, her rescuer's words echoed in her mind.

You'll be okay, Dr. Wilkes.

Even though she'd challenged the man named Jacob Rush, a part of her believed him.

"Head injury," she muttered. Believing people, especially strangers, was a mistake. She'd learned that early in life.

Yet the man with the warm green eyes, crooked smile and firm pectoral muscles outlined through his undershirt seemed so confident in his proclamation.

What had he said? That he'd been a social worker turned full-time father? Of course, being a father to a young girl required one to develop the ability to calm a hysterical child.

Brie had fallen into that category once. She'd been insecure and emotional, almost losing her inquisitive nature to shame and submission. It made sense that Jacob would know how to calm Brie. But was his concern genuine?

Once again, she glanced across the river. Hugging herself, she sensed danger was close but couldn't identify its source. Needing to feel less like a victim and more in control, she shucked the blanket and pulled the sweatshirt over her head.

Rolling up the sleeves, she reached down for her boots, and a wave of dizziness brought her to her knees. The light-headedness triggered another round of anxiety—another symptom of a brain injury. Or was this anxiety about something else? Instinct warning her to beware?

She decided not to wait by the fire like a helpless child. She adjusted the blanket across her shoulders and started up the tree-lined trail where Jacob had gone.

She'd told him she didn't have time for frivolous hikes. Truth was, she couldn't rationalize spending time in nature because there was work to be done in the lab. She picked up her pace, intent on finding Jacob to demand he take her back to town.

What was her current project again? Alternatives to drug therapy for those suffering from autoimmune disease. There, she remembered. She was fine.

As she trudged up the trail, she thought she heard something but couldn't quite identify—

She turned a corner and spotted Jacob on the ground.

A man hovered over him.

She bit back a gasp. The man turned and looked right at her. Before he could utter a word, she took off, stumbling over twigs and rocks on the trail.

"Dr. Wilkes! Don't run!" the man shouted.

Really? He thought her gullible enough to stop because he'd ordered her to do so?

She made it back to the camp and tried mounting Jacob's horse. Since she'd never ridden a horse, she only managed to frustrate the animal. It trotted away, taking with it any chance for escape.

"It's okay," the man said behind her.

She spun around and glared. It was certainly not okay. Her memory might be compromised, but she was fairly sure Jacob was one of the good guys.

The tall man approached her.

She put out her hands, making her position clear—she didn't want him coming any closer. She took a step back…

In a swift motion he lunged and flung her away from the riverbank, hurling her a good six feet. Landing hard on the damp ground, she struggled to breathe, the wind knocked from her lungs.

"I'm sorry, Dr. Wilkes, but I can't risk you falling into the river. I'm Eric, a security officer."

She took a few quick breaths. "What did you do to Jacob?"

"Jacob? You mean the guy up the trail?"

She nodded over her shoulder at him.

"Do you know him?" Eric said.

"He saved my life…pulled me out of the river."

"I think you're confused."

She hated that he was stating the obvious. Still, she knew she wasn't confused about Jacob having saved her life.

"Why do I need security?" she said, angry at his condescending tone.

Angry at her own vulnerability.

"There have been threats against your life, and we were sent to find you."

"We?"

"Me and my partner, Bobby."

"Well, you failed, because I ended up nearly drowning."

"I'm sorry about that, Doctor. What were you doing down by the river?"

"I was…" She suddenly remembered the other man who'd claimed to be with security, how she'd felt threatened by him, his menacing eyes, sinister tone.

"Ma'am?" Eric said.

She needed to develop a sensible strategy until she knew the truth of who were her allies and who were her enemies. Should she attempt to escape this tall, broad-shouldered man, or go along with him to buy time?

The second choice seemed the wisest. She'd act as if she required immediate medical attention. She'd be safe at the hospital, where she could process what had happened, figure out how she'd ended up in the middle of a forest— or rather, floating down a river.

I went from being a social worker with the Detroit PD to being a full-time father of a precocious little girl, and a ranch hand.

That was an incredibly detailed story to create on the spot if Jacob was only pretending. Also, if he'd meant to harm Brie, he wouldn't have bundled her up, built a fire and called for medical aid.

He would have simply kidnapped her. Or worse.

"Doctor?" Eric extended his hand, offering to help her up.

"I… I… My head…" She gripped her head and pretended to faint, hoping to convince him to get her to a hospital.

This action felt passive, but what choice did she have? If the man was truly hired to protect her, he'd seek medical aid, and if he wasn't, well, she was pretty sure he wouldn't want her to die in his custody.

Pretty sure. Not her typical measure of success.

As she lay there, waiting to see what Eric would do, she reviewed what had happened, how she'd lost part of her memory, survived falling into the river and now had seemingly relinquished control to fate.

Fate, not God. Because God didn't exist, not for Brianna.

As she slowed her breathing, she focused on the sound of her surroundings: the crunch of Eric's boots against the ground, the rushing water, an animal calling out in the distance. She needed to prepare herself in case he decided to pick her up. She needed to become dead weight.

An ironic expression given the circumstances.

"Bobby, come in, over," Eric said.

"Eric?"

"I've got her."

Brie didn't dare open her eyes.

"Is she okay?"

"Affirmative. He pulled her out of the river, but I neutralized him."

Neutralized Jacob, that gentle man? Father of a little girl?

"Emergency's been called," Bobby said.

"We can't wait," Eric said. "Meet me by the truck."

She took a slow breath. His next move would be to pick her up.

Seconds stretched like minutes as she prepared herself for what was to come. He gripped her shoulder, and she groaned again for good measure.

"We've gotta go, Doctor."

She wasn't going to make it easy for him.

He leaned her forward to get a better grip...

And suddenly let go with a grunt.

She cracked open her eyes just as his body collapsed on top of her.

"Get off! Get off!" she cried.

Jacob pulled Eric aside and knelt beside her. "Are you okay?"

She nodded. "Yes. But I thought you were... He said he neutralized you."

"We'd better go. Knocking people out isn't my forte, so I'm not sure he'll stay unconscious for long."

With a nod, she started to get up, and he assisted her to a standing position. He quickly tossed snow onto the fire to extinguish it and motioned her toward the trail.

He glanced around. "Where's Star?"

"I scared her off."

He shot her a curious look, reached for her hand and led her toward the trail. He gave her fingers a gentle squeeze. "Are you good with this speed? I mean, how's your head?"

"I also injured my ankle."

He stopped short. "I'm sorry. I didn't know."

"It's manageable. We need to get away from them." She encouraged him to continue walking.

"Them?" he asked.

"There's a second man. They claim to be security officers sent to protect me."

"Why would you need protection?" He grabbed a branch off the ground and offered it to her to assist with walking.

"He said there have been threats against my life, but I'm not sure I believe him."

"Well, if there's a second guy, chances are he'll come over here to meet his buddy."

"Actually, Eric said to meet at the truck."

"Eric?"

"He introduced himself to me."

"Is Eric the man you were talking to on the other side of the river before you fell in?"

"I don't think so."

He shot her a look that she wasn't sure how to interpret. Skepticism, disbelief, perhaps?

"How many guys does it take to guard a doctor of…what are you a doctor of, anyway?"

"Neuroscience."

"So, you're a researcher?"

He made it sound so…one-dimensional. "Sure," she said.

"There's more to it, I know," he said, as if sensing her displeasure that he'd referred to her as a researcher.

"Dr. Wilkes!" a man called.

"We need to get off the trail." Jacob pointed to a cluster of boulders.

They scrambled off the trail and found a spot behind an imposing boulder where they'd be hidden from view. Once out of sight, Jacob put two fingers to his lips to indicate she should stay quiet. Again, he was used to communicating with a child, so she tried not to take offense at the gesture.

"I lost her!" Eric shouted, probably into his radio.

"How…?"

"I was clocked from behind. They couldn't have gone far. They're no doubt headed for town. You follow the trail north and I'll go south. We'll meet in the middle."

"Roger that."

As Brie and Jacob huddled behind the rock, she considered the fact she wasn't much of a huddler or a hand holder. She wasn't comfortable being touched, nurtured, physically soothed, didn't have much experience with it. The few relationships she'd had with men turned sour when it became obvious they expected her to give up her work in order to have children and raise a family.

She didn't have time for that, not when strides could be made to prevent debilitating diseases.

Like the one that took her sister Abigail's life.

A double squeeze of Brie's hand made her look into Jacob's eyes. He whispered, "We're okay."

He must have thought she was worrying about the immediate threat, not her personal losses.

To be polite, she nodded in response. They might be okay for the moment, but once again Jacob couldn't know they were truly okay. After all, three men were hunting her, claiming to be security officers sent to find and protect her.

Everything will be okay.

She'd heard that phrase enough times to realize the words were hollow. But science? Science always provided the truth.

She retrieved her hand from Jacob's and rubbed her hands together, pretending to be cold.

"Dr. Wilkes! I'm trying to help you!" Eric shouted. "I'm trying to keep you from being hurt!"

She pointed to her head wound and raised an eyebrow. Jacob cracked his crooked smile. Brie broke eye contact, needing to focus on the next step—her escape plan from all this danger and drama.

Get back to town.

Get checked out by a doctor.

Get back to work.

Work had always been her driving motivation, her purpose in life: research, find answers, help people.

Why would anyone want to hurt her? They wouldn't, she decided. The man named Eric was lying. But why?

"I can keep you safe!" Eric shouted. "The man you're with could have sent the death threat!"

She snapped her attention to Jacob. He must have sensed her fleeting concern, because he pulled out his wallet and offered it to her. She flipped it open and saw a photograph of Jacob and a small child, a little girl with dark curls, like his. This must be the daughter he'd mentioned.

As Jacob stayed focused on sounds from the supposed security officer, she went through his wallet and noted a charge card, insurance card, auto card and membership card to a supply store. He reached out and thumbed something out of the back pocket: a library card with his picture. He held it up and raised an eyebrow as if to say someone with a local library card couldn't be a shady character.

She replaced the library card and handed him back his wallet.

He didn't need to prove himself. He seemed to be on her side, wanting to keep her safe. If he'd been behind the death threat, he would have let her drown.

Instead, he'd fished her out of the river, was attacked by "Eric" and had lost his horse.

Regardless of Brie's head injury, Jacob's intentions seemed clear: he wanted to help her.

"Dr. Wilkes!" Eric was sounding farther away.

Jacob peered around the boulder. Lowering himself back into position, he whispered, "He's headed north, but let's give it a few more minutes."

"Why are you helping me?" she said softly.

His brows furrowed. "Why wouldn't I help you?"

"I'm a stranger. You shouldn't put your life at risk for a stranger."

"We're all God's children."

"That doesn't answer my question."

"Do I need a reason to help someone?"

"People usually do, yes."

"I didn't want to see you drown." He shrugged. "That's all I got."

"What should we do next?" she said, changing the subject. His answer frustrated her, but she wasn't sure why.

"It would help if I had my horse."

"Oh, sorry."

"What for?"

"I tried to ride her," Brie confessed.

"You have riding experience?"

She shook her head that she did not, the motion causing a burst of pain.

"Gotta give you points for courage."

"Or stupidity."

"Don't be hard on yourself. Survival instinct can make us do crazy stuff. C'mon." He motioned her down from behind the boulder.

She wondered what *crazy* stuff Jacob was referring to.

As they climbed out from their hiding spot, he asked, "How are you feeling? How's your head?"

"Throbbing."

He frowned. "You're in no condition to hike to the trailhead. I'd better find Star."

"She could be anywhere."

"She wouldn't have gone far." He led them back to the area where he'd been assaulted. "My phone's gotta be here somewhere."

As he searched the ground, her gaze scanned the immediate area. Would the men circle around and return?

"Got it." He stood and brushed off his phone. Frowning, he said, "No signal." Then he looked at Brie. "You ready?"

"For what?"

"To move fast. The horse will definitely draw attention to us."

"What horse?"

Jacob brought two fingers to his lips and made a distinctive whistling sound, waited a few seconds and whistled again.

"What are you…?"

The sound of hooves echoed through the woods as Star came trotting toward them.

"Good girl." He patted the horse affectionately, then mounted her. "Use that rock to give yourself a boost," he suggested to Brie.

She climbed onto a rock that added a couple

of feet to her short frame and hoisted herself into the saddle behind him.

"Stop!" a voice called from the distance.

"Hang on, Dr. Wilkes."

Brie wrapped her arms around Jacob's waist. He made a clicking sound, and the horse took off rather abruptly.

Brie held on to Jacob to keep from falling off the back end of the animal. She wouldn't normally cling to a stranger like this, even one with a pleasant demeanor.

This entire day had been anything but normal, and Brie wanted it over.

Concern taunted Jacob, and not only concern about the men trailing them.

His scientist companion had gone oddly quiet.

Thankfully, it seemed they had eluded whoever was after her and had assaulted Jacob. Yet over the course of the last hour, the doctor's conversation had diminished, and her grip around his waist loosened.

He'd kept her talking, peppering her with questions intending to keep her conscious. She'd participated for a while, offering highly articulate responses, then she seemed to grow defensive and asked why Jacob wanted to know so much about her. He confessed he was trying to keep her alert, at which point her answers became clipped and short. She sounded irritated.

She probably considered herself an expert and resented being managed by Jacob, whose education had been about healing the soul, not the physical body.

A neuroscientist. That sounded like an intense career. He wondered what drove her into the field and what her daily routine looked like compared to Jacob's feeding and grooming the horses before his daughter woke, getting her to school, and returning to finish other chores, including food prep for guests, leading a trail ride or general maintenance.

Some days Jacob still couldn't believe how his life had so drastically changed.

Star stumbled, and Dr. Wilkes groaned.

Where were the emergency responders? Jacob should have come across them by now.

"Dr. Wilkes?" he said.

No response.

"Dr. Wilkes?" he said a bit more forcefully.

"Yes?"

"I think you should keep talking."

"About what?"

"Anything, to help you stay conscious."

"I'm tired. And my head hurts."

"I understand. It won't be long now."

"We'll be at the hospital?" she said.

"The trailhead. Emergency will transport you to the hospital."

He prayed they were waiting for him.

"What am I even doing out here?" She sounded utterly frustrated.

"It will come back to you."

"Or maybe not. What if my memory has been compromised in other ways, like…like my work? What if I can't remember…?"

"Slow down, you'll be okay."

"You've said that before, but you have no proof I'll be okay."

She was right, he didn't have any solid proof, but he had faith. Not something that would make her feel better, he assumed.

"I'm sorry," he started. "I'm trying to help you remain calm, because getting worked up only makes a person more anxious. At least that's been my experience with Miri."

"Your daughter."

"Yes."

"How old is she?"

"Five."

"You're comparing my life experience and behavior to that of a five-year-old," she said flatly.

"That practice works for me, too. I mean, telling myself it will be okay. Otherwise, if I let worry get the best of me, I grow more anxious."

"What would you suggest I do to derail my anxiety?"

"Take a slow, deep breath. Maybe say a prayer. Focus on gratitude."

"You sound like a self-help guru."

"I'll take that as a compliment, even though I suspect it wasn't meant that way."

She was quiet for a few seconds. "I... I don't do well with pain, and my head feels like..."

Her grip loosened; her body weight shifted to the right.

He slowed Star and grabbed the doctor's arm as she started to slide off the saddle. He gripped her with both hands and was able to let her drop gently to the ground. He dismounted and knelt beside her.

"Dr. Wilkes? Please open your eyes." As trauma reawakened panic within him, he fought the memory of his failure and focused on the innocent woman lying before him.

Innocent. Like Kara Roberts. Who should have lived but didn't because she'd been caught up in random violence not of her own making, and medics couldn't get to her.

Here he was, facing it again: his inability to save a person's life because he was unable to get help in time.

"Knock it off, Jacob," he muttered. This was not a repeat of the tragedy in Detroit.

This was happening in his new life as a father and rancher. He'd saved this woman from drowning and was doing his best to meet up with EMTs as quickly as possible.

That's all God asks. For us to do our best.

He pressed the back of his hand against her forehead. She was warm, perhaps indicating an infection? His mind started spinning in circles, so he leaned on his faith.

"God, I cast my panic to You," he said softly. "Help me stay calm so I can save this woman's life."

This woman. Dr. Wilkes. He still didn't know her first name.

He took a deep breath and let God's presence fill his heart. "Amen."

With renewed determination, he pulled out his phone and was relieved to see he had a signal.

"Nine-one-one—"

"This is Jacob Rush again. I pulled a woman from the Spruce River. Where's the emergency response team?"

"They're on the way, Jacob."

"How close are they to the Nickelback Trailhead? She just fell unconscious and—"

"It's not right," Dr. Wilkes suddenly said.

She was looking at Jacob with a curious expression like she was someplace else, not out here in the wilderness.

"Hang on," he said to the operator.

"This isn't the data I recorded yesterday," Dr. Wilkes said.

"Dr. Wilkes?"

She looked at Jacob with a confused frown. "Who are you?"

"Jacob Rush, remember?"

"I…" She shook her head, and her eyes widened.

"Hands up and get away from the woman!" a man shouted.

THREE

Jacob pressed the speaker button on his phone, hoping the emergency operator would hear what was happening and send additional help in the form of law enforcement.

"Lemme see your hands!" the assailant repeated.

Dr. Wilkes's eyes widened with fear.

"It's okay." He placed his phone in her hand.

Jacob stood slowly, raised his hands and turned around.

He was facing two male sheriff's deputies. Two EMTs, a man and a woman, stood behind them.

"Oh, good," Jacob said, lowering his hands.

"Hands up!" the younger deputy ordered.

"I'm Jacob Rush, the one who called for help."

"Step away from the woman," the older of the two deputies said.

Jacob took a few steps to his right, wanting nothing more than for them to administer medical aid to Dr. Wilkes. That was his priority.

"Interlace your hands behind your head," the older deputy said. His name badge read Vick.

Jacob did so and calmly said, "I'm not the bad guy here. I pulled Dr. Wilkes out of the river and called 9-1-1. She's suffering from a head injury and an injured ankle. Two men are after her."

As the deputies approached Jacob, Deputy Vick motioned for the medical team to examine Dr. Wilkes.

Finally. Jacob breathed a sigh of relief. At least she was in good hands. He watched the EMTs as the younger of the two deputies searched Jacob for a weapon.

"I'm unarmed," Jacob said.

The younger deputy, whose name badge read Taylor, pulled a knife off Jacob's belt.

"I use that for camping," he explained.

Deputy Taylor continued his search. "That's it," he said, handing Deputy Vick the knife.

"ID is in my back pocket," Jacob offered, keeping his hands behind his head. Deputy Taylor pulled it out and handed it to his partner.

Jacob glanced at Dr. Wilkes, hoping to hear her speak, answer questions, something.

"How long has she been unconscious?" the female EMT asked Jacob.

"She'd just regained consciousness and was speaking when you arrived."

"Mr. Rush?"

Jacob turned to Deputy Vick. "Yes, sir?"

"Why are you out here today?"

"I was on retreat when I heard a woman scream."

"Retreat?"

"Yes, sir."

"What kind of retreat?"

"A spiritual retreat."

Deputy Vick studied him. Police officers tended to be suspicious; it came with the job, both as a tool to assess the danger of a situation and from the experience of seeing folks at their worst. At least that's how Jacob's partner Curt had explained it when Jacob started accompanying Curt on nonemergency calls.

"A background check will show I used to work for the Detroit Police Department as a community service officer."

"Community service?"

"I am—was a social worker," Jacob said. "Now I live at Boulder Creek Ranch with my five-year-old daughter."

"You left your daughter home with your wife?"

"Her mother is deceased. Miri is with her uncle and grandparents, Lacey and Bill Rogers."

Deputy Vick nodded, still wearing a speculative frown.

"Is she conscious?" Deputy Vick asked the female EMT.

"Yes," she answered.

The deputy approached Dr. Wilkes. "Ma'am, do you know this man?" He pointed at Jacob.

Dr. Wilkes studied Jacob as if seeing him for the first time.

"I... I... My head hurts," she groaned.

Jacob's heart clenched at the pain in her voice.

"We need to transport her ASAP," the female EMT said.

"Go ahead," Vick ordered. "We'll get a statement from her at the hospital."

As they carried Dr. Wilkes past, Jacob offered a smile of confidence that she'd be okay, although he knew not to speak the words. She would be okay, or at least she'd be safe at the hospital. Wouldn't she?

Hands still interlaced behind his head, Jacob turned to Deputy Vick. "She could be in danger."

"From who?" he asked.

"The two men I mentioned."

"Who were they?" Vick pressed.

"I don't know. She didn't know, either."

"You'll need to come with us."

The younger deputy pulled handcuffs off his belt.

"Hang on, you're arresting me? For saving a woman's life?"

Deputy Vick motioned the other deputy to stay back, then addressed Jacob. "We need to question you at the station. If you deny our request, we have the right to arrest you."

"For...?"

"Suspicion of kidnapping."

More than two hours later, Jacob was sitting in a conference room at the sheriff's office. He'd been thoroughly questioned, retelling his story twice to Deputy Vick. Then he was left alone. Since he'd given his phone to Dr. Wilkes, Jacob had asked to use the department's phone to call the ranch and let them know what had happened, and that he would be late returning from his trip. Deputy Vick had said he'd find Jacob a phone, then left. That was fifteen minutes ago.

A part of Jacob understood what was going on here. He appreciated the deputy's need to be thorough and piece together who everyone was in this scenario and whom the deputy should believe. Still, if by some supreme accident or misunderstanding Jacob was arrested, his custody of Miri could be threatened. He sensed the Rogers family covertly questioned some of Jacob's decisions. Understandable. They'd been the little girl's primary family for four years until Jacob, a virtual stranger, showed up.

Since he'd moved to Montana over a year ago, he'd done a pretty good job of taking care of his daughter with the family's help, which was a miracle considering how distrustful they were when he'd first arrived. It had taken nearly a year for Jacob's ex-fiancée's brother, Beau, to warm up to him. Jacob had only recently seen a glint of respect in Beau's eyes. He seemed to appreciate both Jacob's efforts to be a good father and his commitment to the family's guest ranch.

Jacob had worked hard for that respect, even though occasionally he sensed distrust from Beau, and Cassie's mother, Lacey. They'd be in each other's lives for a long time thanks to their shared love for Miri, so Jacob did his best to bridge the gap between them.

If only Cassie hadn't abandoned him six years ago when they lived in Detroit. If only she had articulated her concerns to Jacob, maybe they could have worked things out and raised Miri together. Yet back then Cassie knew how singularly focused Jacob had been, devoted to the success of a new community services program. Jacob should have seen how lonely and frustrated Cassie was becoming while he obsessed over helping tortured souls find homes or get into rehab and not end up in jail.

Then there was the death of Kara Roberts, the final straw that must have triggered Cassie's decision to leave. Kara, a teenager, had died in Jacob's arms shattering his faith in humanity and causing him to spew cruel words to Cassie about not wanting to bring children into such an evil world.

Those words drove Cassie away before she'd had a chance to tell him she was pregnant.

The darkness of his job, coupled with Kara's death and Cassie's abandonment had consumed him, almost destroyed him. Then he'd found his faith, which changed the way he viewed life. God gave him hope.

Unfortunately, Cassie was long gone by then. She had claimed to be starting over with a new job in another city, but in reality she'd headed home to Montana and told her family Jacob broke up with her, that he no longer loved Cassie and had no interest in being part of their child's life.

Jacob had tried reaching out to her to apologize and make amends. But his calls would go into voice mail, never to be returned.

For four years he had no idea he was a father.

Jacob had been so consumed with saving the world that he let his own world fall apart.

Was he doing it again? Sabotaging himself by helping a stranger?

No, what he did today was the right thing to do, the Christian thing to do.

The door opened, and Deputy Vick entered the conference room.

"I really need to make that call," Jacob said.

"To an attorney?"

"To check on my daughter."

"I called the ranch to confirm your story."

"You spoke with…?"

"Beau Rogers."

Jacob leaned back in his chair and sighed. He might be warming to Jacob, but Beau was still a cynical man. He'd jump to all kinds of conclusions about why Jacob was being questioned by police.

It seemed obvious that Beau's judgmental nature was born of guilt over his sister's death, that he couldn't protect her. Yet it had been Cassie's choice to get into a car with a drunk driver, a man she'd been casually dating, a man who'd encouraged her to drink alongside him.

"Dr. Wilkes has regained consciousness and confirmed your story," Deputy Vick said.

"She's okay?"

"Seems to be."

Jacob nodded and said a silent prayer of thanks. "Is there anything else you need from me?" he asked Deputy Vick.

"Walk me through what happened one more time."

Practicing patience, Jacob repeated the story for the third time. What would it take for the deputy to believe his story and release him?

Someone knocked on the door, and Deputy Vick cracked it open.

"We have a situation," a female voice said.

"Is he in there?"

Jacob recognized Beau's voice from the hall-way.

"Sir, you need to wait in the lobby," the woman said.

"I want to see him," Beau said.

Deputy Vick opened the door, and Beau charged Jacob, grabbing him by the shoulders and pulling him to his feet. "I'd finally started to trust you!" Beau shouted in Jacob's face.

"I did nothing wrong." Jacob put up his hands in surrender. He wasn't one to fight, especially with family.

Deputy Vick grabbed Beau's arm. "Sir, you need to back off."

"It's okay, Deputy," Jacob said.

"What did you do, Detroit?" Beau accused, using his personal nickname for Jacob instead of his given name.

"I pulled a woman out of Spruce River."

Beau released Jacob and took a step back. "What?"

"She would have drowned."

"You risked your life to save some stranger," Beau said, flatly.

"Yes."

"See, it's stuff like that…" Beau shook his head.

"What?" Jacob countered.

"You can't go risking your life when you have a little girl at home. A good father would have—"

"A good man doesn't let a woman drown. You would have done the same thing."

"Ah, I can't talk to you." Beau threw up his hands and turned away from Jacob.

Jacob didn't appreciate Beau's tone or attitude, nor did he like that Deputy Vick had witnessed the argument.

"Deputy Vick, I need to get home to my daughter," Jacob said.

"Nanna's watching her," Beau said, unable to make eye contact with Jacob.

"She's my responsibility." Jacob was done being treated like a criminal, first by the cops and now by Miri's uncle. He looked at Deputy Vick. "Dr. Wilkes confirmed my story that I saved her, correct?"

"Yes."

"Then I'm leaving."

Jacob started for the door. He shouldn't be penalized for being cooperative and helpful.

The deputy allowed him to pass. "We'll be in touch if we have more questions."

"You know where to find me. Where's my horse?"

"They took him to Grosh Stables. Closed for the day."

"I'll pick her up tomorrow. Don't suppose I could get a ride home?"

"C'mon," Beau grumbled and marched past Jacob out the door.

It was going to be a long night.

Brie was more than a bit overwhelmed. An unusual state and one she loathed.

They'd moved her to a room even though she'd said she'd rather not spend the night in the hospital. Once she was settled, a sheriff's deputy hammered her with questions about what transpired in the mountains, why she was out there, who was after her and how she knew Jacob. She was very clear about the role Jacob played of the Good Samaritan, that he'd saved her life. She didn't know the identity of the other men who claimed to be security officers.

A few minutes after the deputy left, Andrea Carp, university administrator, stopped by. She explained that she'd been contacted by the Viceroy Foundation, cosponsors of Brie's research, who had requested the university assign security to protect Brie until Viceroy's agent arrived in town.

"Wait, so those men, Eric, Stan, Bobby…you sent them?"

"Actually, the officers I sent were unable to find you."

"Then who were those three men in the mountains? And why am I in danger again?" Brie said.

"Your office received threatening emails. Your

research partner, Douglas, notified the foundation, and the foundation contacted us."

Brie nodded, puzzling over why anyone would want to harm her. Surely not for her research into natural ways to reduce inflammation and heal autoimmune disease. What possible enemies could she attract by trying to help more than twenty million Americans who struggled with a condition where the body attacks itself?

"Well, at least I was able to present the workshop on collaboration," Brie said.

"The evaluations were glowing."

"Good to hear."

"What we wouldn't give to have someone like you on our staff."

"Thank you."

"Anyway, I'd better let you rest."

Brie had no interesting in resting. She wanted out of this place. It triggered too many dreadful memories of visiting her sister, watching her mother cry and seeing her father's broken expression.

"I appreciate you coming by," she said to Andrea.

"You're welcome. I'm sending one of our security officers to the hospital to keep an eye on things."

"Thanks, but I plan to leave as soon as possible."

"Do you think that's wise?"

"I've been diagnosed with a concussion and a sprained ankle. Nothing that requires hospitalization, although the concussion will prevent me from getting on a plane for a few days."

"I'll extend your reservation at the motel."

"Thank you."

Andrea started to leave.

"Andrea?"

"Yes?"

"Do you know why I went into the mountains today?"

"You said something about practicing one of your protocols."

Perhaps, the healing balm of forest bathing?

As Andrea approached the door, the sound of a muted phone rang from the closet. Andrea turned to her. "Should I...?"

"Yes, please."

Andrea opened the closet door and pulled a phone out of a bag of Brie's things.

It wasn't Brie's phone. Then she remembered Jacob had given it to her.

"Call me if you need anything," Andrea said with a pleasant smile, and left.

Brie eyed the phone. The image of a smiling girl popped up on the screen. Brie hit the accept button.

"Papa Jay?" a little girl's voice said, before Brie could speak.

"No, this is Dr. Wilkes."

"A doctor? What's wrong with my daddy?" the little girl croaked.

"Nothing, he's fine. I'm his…friend. He should be home soon."

"Promise?"

"Yes," Brie said, because it had been obvious how much Jacob loved his daughter.

How could she know that fact when she'd only met the man earlier today?

The sound of heavy breathing filled the line.

"Hello?" Brie said.

"I want my daaaa-ddy," she said, her voice trembling.

"I know. He'll come home soon."

"Where i-i-i-is he?"

"I'm not sure."

"Then how do you know he's coming ho-o-o-ome?"

"Because I know how much he loves you."

"Why did he leave me?" she sobbed, and the line went dead.

The child's desperate cries for her father twisted Brie's gut into a knot. He wasn't home with his daughter, and it was most likely Brie's fault. She was told by Deputy Taylor that they were questioning Jacob at the station. She had to get to him, tell Jacob that his daughter needed him.

Like Brie had needed her father all those years ago after he'd abandoned her.

She pulled the IV out of her hand and went to the closet. She got dressed, slipping on her jeans, T-shirt and Jacob's sweatshirt with the Boulder Creek Ranch logo on the front.

She stepped out of her room and looked both ways. No university security officer. Unfortunate, since she could use a ride to the police station.

Brie made haste and rushed to the stairs before anyone could detain her.

The only thing that mattered was finding Jacob.

She was walking pretty well on the sprained ankle, probably due to the mild pain meds they'd given her to dull the ache.

She went to the elevator and pressed the down button. It seemed to take forever.

Why did he leave me? The little girl's voice haunted her.

Spotting the Exit sign, she decided to take the stairs instead. She opened the door and started down, suddenly wondering if the concussion and pain meds were messing with her cognitive function. Perhaps it wasn't the best idea to be putting so much pressure on her ankle if she expected it to heal. They'd given her crutches, but she'd left them in the room. No time to go back now.

One flight down, almost there.

Once she reached the main floor, she'd order a

cab to take her to the police station. Then again, couldn't she just call?

Why did he leave me?

Brianna felt the child's pain. She'd lived that pain.

She flung open the door to the first floor and was hyperfocused on the red Exit sign in the distance. Nothing else mattered.

As she headed down the hall, someone suddenly blocked her.

Stan.

The man from the mountains with the wicked smile.

She stepped back.

He grabbed her arm. "No, ma'am. This time you're coming with me."

FOUR

At first Jacob had been hesitant to ask his brother-in-law to swing by the hospital, because he didn't want to irritate Beau even more. But Jacob needed his phone, and truth be told, he wanted to check on Dr. Wilkes. He hoped she was still at the hospital, that she hadn't left against doctor's orders. Jacob knew how some people reacted when they felt frightened or helpless: they ran.

Kind of like Cassie.

"We've got a campfire booked after dinner tonight," Beau said.

He was back to focusing on business. It was easier for a guy like Beau to talk business, not emotions or frustrations. When Beau confronted his own frustration, he tended to blow up. A few times in the past year, Jacob had come close to asking Beau pointed questions to encourage him to open up. Instead, Beau would shut down, accusing Jacob of "shrinking" him.

Jacob had only been trying to help. Instead of using therapist tools, he decided to pray for Beau, pray that the pain of whatever anger and guilt he carried would be eased by God's love. That's all Jacob could do.

"Did you hear me?" Beau challenged.

"I did." He turned to Beau. "Campfire after dinner. I'll be there to help."

"Will you?"

"Look, Beau—"

"Don't start. You can't convince me what you did today was a good idea, not for a father of a young child like Miri."

"I didn't feel I had a choice."

"We always have a choice, Detroit. You chose to meddle in someone else's dangerous business, and it could've gotten you killed."

There was shame in his tone, shame and fear.

"I saved a woman's life," Jacob said. "I did not know about the danger that would follow."

Beau loved his niece and had loved his sister. He was probably haunted not only by Cassie's death but also by the possibility of Miri suffering that kind of loss again.

Jacob understood Beau's fear, even if he didn't appreciate the tone.

"Nothing has changed, Beau. I'm committed to the family, the ranch…but most of all I'm committed to my daughter."

"Then why aren't we going straight home?"

"I need to get my phone."

"You sure that's all it is?"

"Meaning?"

"Meaning, maybe your hero complex is flaring up again."

Hero complex? Jacob shook his head and gazed out the passenger window. A true hero would have been able to save Kara Roberts's life.

A true hero wouldn't have driven Miri's mother away.

Jacob would be the first to admit he'd experienced the savior complex in the past, but he'd shucked that mindset when he found himself on his knees, his world crashing down around him.

They pulled up to the hospital, and Beau parked.

"I'll be right back," Jacob said.

"I'm coming with you."

Jacob got out of the car, feeling like a child being accompanied by a distrustful dad. Perhaps Beau wanted to form his own opinion about the stranger who had inadvertently put Jacob's life at risk. It was probably curiosity that motivated Beau to stick close to Jacob.

Or was he shadowing Jacob to make sure he didn't make another poor decision?

They entered the hospital, and Jacob noticed Meredith Hamm behind the reception desk. Jacob reconsidered Beau's motivation. It was pretty obvious Meredith had a thing for Beau.

"Hi, Jacob. Hi, Beau." Her eyes lit up when she said his name.

Beau nodded but didn't return the greeting.

"I'm looking for a patient, last name Wilkes," Jacob said.

Meredith cast a smile Beau's way, but he was scanning the lobby.

"First name?" Meredith said.

"I don't know her first name," Jacob said.

Beau shot him a look.

Jacob shrugged. "She introduced herself as Dr. Wilkes."

That got another head shake from Beau.

"Let's see, Brianna Wilkes, room 203."

Brianna. A beautiful name.

Beau turned and walked toward the elevator. Jacob shot Meredith a consolatory nod and followed him.

"Hang on," Jacob said as he caught up to Beau. "Just because you're angry with me doesn't mean you have to be rude to Meredith."

"I wasn't rude."

"Yeah, you were. It's like watching someone yell at a puppy."

"What's that supposed to mean?"

"It's cruel, Beau. She's crazy about you, and you ignore her. If you're not interested, tell her, but you don't have to be boorish."

"I don't even know what that means."

"Look it up."

"Listen, smart guy—"

"Let me go!" a woman's voice echoed from the stairwell.

Instincts kicked in, and Jacob took off toward the sound, Beau right behind him.

Jacob pushed the door open into the stairs.

"Where…?"

Jacob put up his hand to silence Beau. They waited a few seconds. Jacob looked up, and down. Didn't see anyone.

The slam of a door rebounded from below. The garage.

"C'mon." Jacob practically sprinted down the stairs to the basement. When he reached the exit door, Beau grabbed his shoulder.

"Slow down. You don't know what we're walking into," Beau said.

Jacob took a breath to calm his adrenaline and glanced at Beau. He nodded, and Jacob opened the door.

"What do you want?" Brianna cried.

"I want you to stop fighting me," a male voice said.

Beau pointed one way and nodded for Jacob to go the other. Jacob crouched out of sight behind a car and stealthily made his way along the right side of the parking garage. Beau disappeared around the opposite side.

"I said let me go! Somebody help…!"

A slapping sound bounced off the cars.

Brianna whimpered.

And Jacob lost it. He sprung to his feet. "Dr. Wilkes!" he called.

"Jacob!"

Jacob turned toward the sound and spotted Brianna and her abductor in the far corner by the exit gate. He sprinted toward them not knowing what he'd do if the guy had a gun, if he threatened Brianna with it or even shot Jacob. Beau would never let him live that down.

"Release her!" Jacob demanded.

Head down, the guy picked up his pace, pulling Brianna with him as she limped on her injured ankle. Out of nowhere, Beau slid across the hood of a car and slammed into the guy. With a jerk he released Brianna, and she collapsed.

The kidnapper slugged Beau and took off. Beau's face lit bright red with fury. He turned to Jacob and Brianna, debating.

"Go!" Jacob said, knowing Beau didn't want to let the guy get away, especially after getting off that punch.

Beau raced after the kidnapper, and Jacob knelt beside Brianna, her eyes pinched shut.

"Hey, you're safe," Jacob said.

She wouldn't open her eyes at first, and he feared she'd hit her head again, adding more trauma to an already injured brain.

"Are you sure?" she said. Then her beautiful brown eyes opened. Relief tempered his adrenaline.

"Positive," he said. "He's gone."

She sighed, and he offered to help her sit up. Her hand was cold and trembled slightly.

"You're here again," she said.

"I came to get my phone, and to see how you were doing."

"I've been better," she said wryly.

"What happened? Did he kidnap you from your room?"

"No, I was leaving when he caught me."

"The doctor discharged you?"

"No, I had to find you."

Okay, that was really not what he'd expected her to say.

"Because…you wanted to thank me again?" He offered a slight smile.

"Is that flirting? Are you flirting with me?"

She was serious and seemed a peeved. "Uh… sorry, sometimes I joke my way through an uncomfortable situation, and it falls flat."

"You're uncomfortable? Because of me?"

"No. Maybe? I don't know. You said you were looking for me. I didn't expect that."

She started to get up, and he offered a helping hand.

"Your daughter," she said, leaning against a nearby car.

"Miri? What about her?"

"She called." Brianna handed him the phone. "She sounded upset. I tried to case her worry, but I probably said the wrong thing. I'm not good with children."

"I'm sure she's fine. We need to report what happened to the police."

"You need to call your daughter."

"I will. After we—"

"You didn't hear her voice. She's terrified and sad and…and she needs her father," she said, her voice rising in pitch.

"Okay…"

"I don't understand how you can ignore her when she's desperate to talk to you."

"I'll call her in a minute. But right now, we've got to deal with your situation."

Her eyes welled with tears. She blinked, and a tear spilled over and trailed down her cheek.

"Hey, hey." He automatically pulled her against his chest. It felt natural to comfort this woman. And for a few seconds, the world seemed to settle a bit.

A man cleared his throat behind them. Brianna pushed away, and her cheeks were flushed. Was she embarrassed? Or upset with him for, in her mind, breaching her personal space?

Jacob turned to Beau, who wiped blood from his lip with the back of his hand.

"Whoa, you all right?" Jacob said.

"He's got a sneaky right cross. Sorry, ma'am, but I lost him."

Brianna nodded, casting her gaze downward. She looked so forlorn, lost.

"We should get you back to your room," Jacob said.

"No, I'm not going back inside."

"Maybe the police could—"

"I can't stay in the hospital. I just…can't."

"Then how about we give you a ride somewhere?" Beau offered.

"My motel, please."

She'd been through a lot, and Jacob didn't like the idea of her being alone, stalked and continuously threatened.

"I have another idea." Jacob shot Beau a look. Beau nodded his approval. "We'll take you back to the ranch for dinner. It's all-you-can-eat BBQ tonight."

"I am rather hungry," she said, still not making eye contact.

"Great, it's settled."

As she rode with Jacob and Beau to their ranch, Brianna reflected on how she wasn't in the habit of relying on others. On the contrary— she avoided it at all costs, knowing that relying on someone was a foolish habit, one that would leave you vulnerable and heartbroken.

Tonight, she had little choice. It made more

logical sense to accept the gracious offer to accompany Jacob and Beau back to their ranch, where she would get sustenance, thereby stabilizing her blood sugar and giving her the ability to think more clearly.

Because after everything that had happened today, she felt beyond rattled. Some might say she even bordered on unstable.

Stop that crying. You have a roof over your head and hot meals. You have no right to cry.

The memory of her aunt's voice echoed in Brianna's brain. Maybe for her next project she'd figure out how to erase past memories and childhood trauma from the hippocampus. The odd thing was, she hadn't thought about Aunt Judith, the woman her dad had sent her to live with after he remarried, and her shaming tone in years. Which meant this current direction of thought was triggered by Brie's brain injury. She knew enough about brain trauma to expect possible cognitive challenges, emotional outbursts and even confusion.

"Here we are," Jacob said from the front seat.

Beau pulled up to a rather large house with a wraparound porch, tall picture window and front door with a wooden sign hanging above that read Welcome.

As Jacob opened his car door, a little girl sprinted from the house, squealing. "Papa Jay! Papa Jay!"

Brie got out of the car and watched the child launch herself into Jacob's arms.

A knot twisted in Brie's chest. She took a calming breath and tried to appreciate the moment, instead of reliving that which she sorely missed.

"Hey, kiddo. You have a good day at school?" Jacob asked.

"We made pine-cone animals!"

"You did? What kind?"

"All kinds. Greta Hill made dogs, Nicky Anderson made owls and Vivian made baboons." The little girl snickered.

Beau stepped around the front of the SUV, watching the interaction with a melancholy expression.

"Hi, Papa Beau-Beau."

"Hey, munchkin," he said in a gentle voice.

"What kind of animal did *you* make?" Jacob asked his daughter.

"Guess."

"Let's see… A flamingo?"

"No," she said with a giggle.

"A kangaroo?"

Miri shook her head.

"A pig!" Jacob snorted in Miri's ear, and she burst out laughing.

The sound made Brie smile.

"Papa Jay, stop!" Miri said.

"I give up. What did you make?"

"An owl, of course!"

Beau glanced at the ground and sighed.

"Of course," Jacob said, his voice softer than before.

"You wanna see?"

"You know it."

She jumped down and pulled him toward the house.

"Hang on. This is my friend," Jacob said, trying to introduce Brie.

But the little girl was on a mission and kept pulling him away. "Your friend can come. And you, too, Papa Beau-Beau."

"Right behind you," Beau said.

Jacob and Miri disappeared in the house.

"I'm not good at reading subtext," Brie said to Beau. "But you seem upset." She wanted to know why the mention of an owl had such an impact on the men and why the child called them both Papa.

Beau motioned her toward the house. "The owl was her mother's thing. She collected them, gave Miri a wooden owl on her fourth birthday. Miri named him Edgar. It was the last birthday Miri had with her mom."

Brie looked at him in question.

"Her mom, my sister, died in a car accident over a year ago."

"Oh, I'm so sorry," Brie said.

"Thanks."

Brie gazed at the house, all lit up. "That must have been devastating for the child."

"Yeah, although Miri spent more time here with us than with her mom."

Brie frowned in question.

"Cassie had a job in town and only made it out here on the weekends—most weekends."

"And Jacob was…?"

"Back in Detroit. I'll let him tell you that part."

He had abandoned his daughter?

They reached the front door and swung it open. Brie froze at the sight of a rather large group of people filling the great room. Their voices drifted up to the high ceiling, wood beams stretched from one end of it to the other. It was like nothing she'd ever seen before, straight out of a mountain life magazine. On the far wall was a rock-faced fireplace; burning logs cast a welcoming glow across the room.

It's like she'd walked into another world.

"Mom, this is Brianna Wilkes," Beau said. "Brianna, this is my mom, Lacey Rogers."

Brianna was greeted by a blonde woman in her sixties wearing a dark green button-down shirt, jeans and cowboy boots. "Welcome, Brianna. Beau didn't tell me he was dating anyone."

"She's not with me. She's a friend of Jacob's."

"Actually, Jacob pulled me out of the river," Brianna corrected.

"Wow," Lacey said with a slight chuckle. "Well, how about some hot cider or coffee?"

"I'd hate to put you out. Looks like you've got a lot going on." Brie eyed the room.

"After a few days at the ranch, our guests are like family. They're pretty much self-serve kinds of folks. I'll be right back with…?"

"Cider would be lovely, thank you."

Jacob and Miri crossed the room. "Papa Beau, look!" Miri held up a pine-cone owl with big, round eyes, flat ears and a pointed nose.

"That's fantastic, kid."

"Thank you." She blinked her big green eyes and held it up for Brianna to inspect.

Brianna knelt and took a closer look. "I especially like the big eyes. Did you know owls don't have eyes like us?"

Miri shook her head and looked at her owl's eyes, then back at Brianna.

"They're not eyeballs, exactly. They're more like tubes. Although they have great night vision and can see things far away, they have trouble seeing things up close. And get this—they have three eyelids."

"Three? What for?"

"One for blinking, one for sleeping and one for keeping their eye tubes clean."

"Did you hear that, Papa Jay? Three eyelids," Miri said, awe in her voice. "I gotta tell Gramps."

Miri ran off into the group toward an older gentleman with gray hair and a broad smile.

"I'd better check on the horses," Beau said and excused himself.

Brie straightened, wincing against the ache of her sprained ankle.

"What's wrong? You dizzy? Need to sit down? I'll get you some cheese," Jacob said.

"Thanks. I'm not dizzy, but I think I will sit down."

He motioned to a nearby chair and she sat down. She gazed across the group of guests, puzzled by the connection she witnessed.

"These people are not related?" she asked Jacob.

"Nope, they met for the first time earlier this week."

A couple of men listened to a third man tell a story, then the three of them burst out laughing.

"You look perplexed," Jacob said.

"I don't have a lot of social connections." To stop him from pitying her, she clarified, "I'm dedicated to my work."

He offered an odd expression she couldn't interpret.

"I understand," he said.

She snapped her attention back to the group. How could he possibly understand if Brie didn't understand why she was destined to be alone?

"If it's too much stimulation, I could set you up in the den with the TV remote," Jacob offered.

She looked at him. "I don't watch television."

"Right, well, there are books in there, too, although probably none by Oliver Sacks or Freud."

"You're joking? I made you uncomfortable again?"

"No, I..." Jacob sighed and shook his head.

"Here's your cider," Mrs. Rogers said, approaching them with a glass cup. The grayhaired man walked up beside her. "This is my husband, Bill Rogers."

"Nice to meet you," he said.

"Bill, can you check on the corn?"

"Sure, hon." He kissed her cheek and went into the kitchen.

A knock sounded at the front door. As Lacey went to answer, she said, "Jacob, Brianna looks a little pale. Why don't you get her some cheese?"

Brie and Jacob shared a knowing smile.

"Are you sure you don't want some cheese?" he said.

"Maybe in a minute," Brie said. "But first, I'd like you to tell me something."

"Anything in particular?" He nodded at a passing guest, a female in her thirties.

Brie felt a sting of jealousy. Odd.

"Why did you abandon your little girl?" Brianna said.

He snapped his attention to her. "Excuse me?"

It was the first time Brie had seen him…not angry, exactly, but offended, maybe even hurt.

"Beau said you arrived in Montana after Miri's mother died."

"I would have been here sooner if I'd known I had a daughter."

"Your wife didn't tell you?"

"She wasn't my wife, and no, she didn't tell me she was pregnant when she left me. I found out I had a child a little over a year ago, the same day I was notified of Cassie's death."

When her gaze caught his, she couldn't look away no matter how much she wanted to. The pain she read in his green eyes triggered shame in her chest. She'd caused that anguish with her impertinent question.

"Brianna?" Mrs. Rogers said.

Brie ripped her attention from Jacob and caught the older woman's worried frown.

"Detective Harper is here to speak with you. I put him in the den for privacy." Mrs. Rogers motioned for her to follow, but Jacob interceded.

"I'll take her."

He offered his hand, and Brie took it. She felt it rude not to, and she could use a little support. Between the brain trauma and injured ankle, she didn't want to risk losing her footing and going down in front of all these people.

"Dinner will be served in half an hour," Mrs.

Rogers said with a curious wrinkle of her eyebrows.

Jacob led Brie out of the great room, down a long hallway.

"I'm sorry if I offended you," she said.

"You didn't."

"Then why do I sense you're upset with me?"

"Not with you. The situation in general—the choices my ex-fiancée made."

"You were going to be married?"

"We were. Then she was gone. She left me right after she found out she was pregnant." He hesitated in front of a door. "I'm here for Miri now. That's what counts."

He knocked twice and opened the door.

"Ma'am, I'm Detective Harper," the officer introduced himself.

"If you need me, I'm right out here," Jacob said to Brie and shut the door.

Jacob wasn't sure how the interview went with Detective Harper, but Dr. Wilkes—Brianna—seemed even more reserved than usual afterward. She'd barely spoken during dinner.

Maybe it was the boisterous nature of the group. These particular guests blended especially well, making friendships that would last past checkout. Some had even scheduled return visits to meet up at the ranch next year.

Another blessing of living here and helping with the ranch had been watching complete strangers come together to develop lasting friendships. It helped confirm Jacob's faith in mankind and his faith in community. Humans weren't meant to be alone and isolated. They were meant to work together, worship together and laugh together.

Brianna Wilkes hadn't laughed at all tonight. She'd cracked a smile when Miri told an animated story, but other than that, Jacob had no idea what was going on in her mind. He sensed her brain was working overtime, speculating, analyzing, concluding.

He wondered what she'd decided about the group of guests, and his family.

His family. It felt amazing thinking of them that way. He only hoped they were growing comfortable with the idea of Jacob being around for a long time.

After dinner, Brianna asked for a ride back to her motel. She said her foundation was sending a bodyguard, thereby releasing Jacob from any responsibility he felt to protect her.

She made it sound like a business deal or obligation on his part, which was not the case. But he didn't want to get into the nuances of what service to others meant and why it was important, because neither of them had the energy for the discussion that would probably turn into an argument. Jacob helped people because it was the right thing to do, whereas Brianna seemed to think there had to be a motivation behind offering help.

At any rate, Jacob knew better than to try and convince her to stay at the ranch. He sensed her need to make her own decisions and to have those decisions respected by others.

Beau offered to read to Miri before bed, so Jacob drove Brianna back to town.

The car ride was painfully quiet.

Even his counseling skills seemed inadequate in this situation. When in doubt, try small talk.

"What'd you think of the barbecue?"

"It was delicious. Thank you very much."

Another few minutes of silence.

"You sure you don't want to swing by the hospital and—"

"No!" she said rather loudly.

He shot her a quick glance, then refocused on the road.

"I don't like hospitals."

Her tone sounded like a child's.

"Bad experience, huh?" he said.

She narrowed her eyes at him.

"Wild guess," he clarified lightly.

"I spent a lot of time visiting my sister in the hospital when I was young."

"Oh, I'm sorry." He waited to see if she would share more. When she didn't, he changed the subject.

"When do you plan to return home? Where is home, anyway?"

"Chicago. I won't be traveling for a few days. It is unwise to fly with a concussion."

"I wanted to thank you for giving Miri the scoop on owls. She was really impressed with the whole three-eyelid thing."

"Your daughter is very bright."

"I'd like to think so, but I'm her dad, so my opinion doesn't count."

"Does my opinion count?"

"Sure."

"She is curious, persistent and uses well-developed critical thinking skills. She's going to go far in whatever career she chooses to pursue."

"As long as she's happy," he said softly.

They pulled up to her motel.

"You don't have to—"

"I'll make sure your bodyguard is in place before I leave," he interrupted.

He exited the truck and went around to open her door. She still seemed unsteady, so he offered his hand. She ignored it and straightened, chin held high like she was proving she didn't need his help, didn't need anyone's help.

They entered the motel and approached the front desk. A young woman nodded her greeting.

"I'm Dr. Brianna Wilkes. Did the university contact you about extending my stay?"

The young woman typed something on a keyboard. "Yes, we have you staying for another four days. You'll need a new key card. Here." She programmed a key card and handed it to Brianna. "The university sent a basket of food, and we put it in your room."

"Thank you."

Jacob escorted Brianna through the lobby, where he noted a middle-aged man and woman sharing a drink while watching a football game on a big-screen TV. Other than the couple, the place was quiet.

"I really can manage from here," she said.

"I know."

"But you're not leaving."

"No, ma'am. When is your bodyguard supposed to arrive?"

"I'm not sure. I'll have to call from the room, since I lost my cell phone."

"We should get you a new phone tomorrow."

"I'll manage, thank you."

She was being polite, but he knew she wanted to say, "Leave me alone," while he wanted to convince her it was appropriate to accept help from a stranger. Although they were feeling less like strangers in Jacob's mind. She'd met his daughter and surrogate family. She knew things about him no other woman knew, like how he'd failed Cassie so miserably that she had abandoned him.

"I'm around the corner by the ice machine,"

she said as they reached a dead end. They turned left…

And saw two men fighting in the hallway. He instinctively shifted Brianna behind him to keep her safe.

"Where is she? Where is Dr. Wilkes!"

FIVE

Jacob gently but quickly led Brianna back around the corner and into the public ladies' bathroom. He encouraged her to enter a stall with him, and he shut and locked the door behind them. He climbed up on the toilet seat in case the guy came looking for Brianna in the women's bathroom, although that seemed unlikely, since he hadn't seen Jacob and Brianna.

No, the assailant was too intent on beating up the other man to discover Brianna's location.

Jacob called Emergency. "This is Jacob Rush," he whispered. "Assault and battery at Wildwood Motel."

He ended the call. That's all they needed to know, and Jacob wanted to stay quiet and focused, not draw unnecessary attention to the bathroom.

Brianna hugged herself and watched him with a look of disbelief, as if to say, *How could this be happening again?* A good question but one for which he had no answer.

His only thought was protecting this woman from violent men.

Lord, give me the wisdom to make the best choices.

Kind of ironic considering he was hiding out in a ladies' bathroom.

The bathroom door swung open. Jacob placed a calming hand on Brie's shoulder. She looked up into his eyes, and he offered a nod of assurance. The only way the guy could physically get to them was to climb under the stall, and Jacob would be waiting.

Soft humming echoed off the tile walls.

Jacob exhaled. It wasn't the attacker.

A phone rang. "Hey, Kirstin… When?… Sure, I can do that." The bathroom door slammed shut.

Brianna sighed, hugging herself.

"Police will be here soon," Jacob whispered.

"And then what?" she said.

"Shh, whisper."

"I'm tired of hiding out." She unlocked the stall door.

"Brianna." He placed his hand against the door to keep it shut.

"This is ridiculous. I am behaving like a child."

"Please lower your voice."

"You need to let me go."

He studied her, this smart, obviously well-educated neuroscientist, and realized it was probably her brain trauma causing this reaction to a terrifying situation.

"I can't stop you, but if you put yourself at risk, you're putting me at risk. I have a little girl waiting for me at home, so I'd ask that you consider her over yourself." He felt badly using a Miri guilt trip but didn't know what else to say to get through to her.

She pursed her lips. "I didn't ask you to protect me."

"That is true."

"You could leave me here and go back to your daughter."

"Yes, I could."

Jacob was trying to deescalate the conflict rather than stoke the flame.

"Can you do this one last thing for me?" he whispered. "Stay here with me until the police arrive?"

"And then?"

"I'll leave you alone, if that's what you want."

She nodded in agreement, but he could tell she wasn't happy about his request.

Making unwise decisions wasn't unusual for someone with a brain injury, so Jacob wrote her behavior off and hoped she wouldn't hold him to the whole "I'll leave you alone" comment, because he'd be hard-pressed to leave her behind tonight.

A plan was already forming in his mind, a plan to take her back to the ranch for her own protection.

The man frustrated Brie beyond words.

Yet he also calmed her with his soft, pleading tone.

How was that possible? Was it his voice or his seemingly sincere countenance?

Or was the brain injury affecting her perceptions? It truly wasn't very smart to leave the bathroom stall, their temporary hiding spot that seemed to offer safety. Not smart at all, she realized. His refusal to let her go triggered a plethora of emotions from her childhood.

Being bossed around, dictated to.

Controlled.

That burst of emotion sprang to the surface when he placed his hand on the bathroom door to prevent her from leaving.

For her own good. He was protecting her, she realized.

And she was angry about it.

She needed sleep, needed to feel safe and not fear someone was going to pop out of the shadows and...

Clarity suddenly hit her. "That was him," she whispered. "Stan from the river."

"Beating up the guy in the hallway?"

She nodded.

"And the other man?"

Brianna shook her head. She had no idea who the other man was or why he was being beaten by Stan.

Jacob's phone vibrated. "Jacob Rush."

He eyed Brianna. "We'll be right there." He pocketed his phone. "Police have arrived."

She unlocked the stall door, and they stepped out.

He touched her shoulder. "Do you need a minute?"

"No, I'm good."

They exited the bathroom. When Jacob motioned her left, toward her motel room, she paused.

"It's safe. Police are waiting for us by your room." Jacob offered his hand.

When she didn't immediately take it, he withdrew his hand and motioned her forward. They headed down the hall, where she saw a deputy and two EMTs, who were tending to the beating victim. One of the EMTs moved aside, giving Brianna a clear view of the stranger.

Her heart lurched at the sight of his injuries: his face was bruised, blood smeared his hand as he gripped his ribs and his eye was starting to swell.

That could have been her.

"I'm Jacob Rush, and this is Brianna Wilkes," Jacob said to a deputy.

"You're Dr. Wilkes?" the injured man said, looking directly at Brianna.

"Yes."

"I was sent by the Viceroy Foundation to protect you." He shrugged. "Sorry, I obviously failed."

"No need to apologize. I'm fine."

The man nodded but didn't look satisfied.

"Brianna?"

She turned to Jacob, who stood next to Detective Harper, the man who'd questioned her earlier at the ranch.

"Ma'am," Detective Harper greeted.

"Detective. I'd like to get my things." She started for the doorway.

Jacob blocked her. "You shouldn't go in there."

She stepped around him and froze at the sight of clothes strewn everywhere, contents of her cosmetics bag littering the floor and the bed linens stripped away. An act of rage had caused this scene. She had no doubt.

Her gaze caught on her favorite blue cashmere sweater, sliced in half. What had the culprit been looking for? She scanned the room, and something seemed odd. No computer or computer bag. Had she brought one? She couldn't remember. She might have left it at home. The university had plenty she could use.

"C'mon," Jacob said, leading her back out.

He and Detective Harper accompanied her down the hall into a conference room.

Detective Harper shut the door. "We're going to dust the room for prints, although the vic said the assailant was wearing gloves."

"What does he want?" Brianna said softly.

Detective Harper sat at the conference table and motioned for her to join him. Jacob stood off to the side.

"Perhaps this has to do with your research?" the detective said.

"We're not that close to publishing our findings. And what would they gain by hurting me?"

"Who benefits from your research?"

"About twenty-three million people."

Detective Harper eyed her in question.

"My research involves calming the body's autoimmune response to diseases like lupus, multiple sclerosis and rheumatoid arthritis, using natural protocols as opposed to external intervention."

"External intervention?"

"Pharmaceuticals. My focus is to trigger the body's healing system to turn off its inappropriate immune response, to stop it from attacking itself."

"The man this evening, he was the same assailant who initially tried to harm you in the mountains?"

"Yes, he called himself Stan."

"I'll put out a description and contact your foundation tomorrow for more details about threats they've received. I'd advise you not to stay at the motel."

"I'll check with the family," Jacob said.

"What family?" Brie said.

"You could stay at the ranch."

"And bring trouble to those nice people? No, thank you. I'd rather leave town."

"I'd prefer you stay close to help us with the case," Detective Harper said. "The ranch is a good option."

"They found me in the mountains and at the motel. What makes you think…?"

"You were probably followed into the mountains, and you were registered under your name at the motel," Jacob said. "They're looking for Dr. Brianna Wilkes, not Sara Clark."

"Who is Sara Clark?"

"The ranch's new guest services assistant." He nodded at the detective. "I'll double-check with the family, but I'm sure they'll be onboard."

"Don't I have a say in this?" Brie asked.

Both men looked at her. Waited.

She sighed. What other option did she have?

"I suppose it's the best strategy. For now."

Something kept niggling at Brianna's brain on their way back to the ranch. The detective's question about her work being the reason behind the multiple kidnapping attempts.

Her work. She'd barely given it much thought since she'd fallen into the river. And now, as she gazed out the passenger window into the dark expanse of the Montana countryside, she realized she couldn't remember specifics about her current research other than the broad strokes.

Her hands began to tremble, so she interlaced her fingers in her lap. A good night's sleep was what she needed, that and to feel safe so she could effectively calm her sympathetic nervous system response.

It must have been the combination of head trauma and the adrenaline coursing through her body that shut down some of her memories and affected her cognitive function. She'd fully recover and remember. The swelling in her brain would ease, and it would all come back to her.

But what if it didn't?

"If you were anyone else, I'd think you were praying," Jacob said.

She looked at him. He nodded toward her hands, gripped securely in her lap.

"I'm thinking." She unclenched her fingers.

"Sometimes a good thing. Sometimes not." He winked.

She snapped her gaze from his. How did this man seem to read her thoughts, know her feelings, when most people struggled to simply understand her?

"Anything I can help with?" he said.

"You've done more than enough, but thank you." She looked at him again. "I'm surprised your family agreed to this."

"Why?"

She shrugged, realizing somewhere, deep down, she'd assumed they would not consider her worth the risk, not worth the effort.

"They are good people who believe in taking care of one another and offering a helping hand to a stranger. Although you're not really a stranger."

"What am I?"

"What do you mean?"

"I'm not a friend. You didn't know me until you pulled me out of the river today."

"True. It was a good thing I happened by when I did."

"Coincidence."

"Was it?"

"You're suggesting…?"

"I think God presents us with opportunities."

"So, I'm not a stranger, I'm not a friend, I'm an opportunity."

"No. You're a woman who needs help."

She turned away from him and stared at the road ahead.

"Why does that bother you so much?" he asked. "The thought of needing help?"

"I'm independent."

"So am I, but I don't mind accepting help from time to time. I need help raising my daughter. I needed help learning the skills of a rancher."

"That's not the same as what I'm going through."

"Help is help. No matter what form it takes."

"Well, usually I don't need it, nor do I accept it. From anyone."

"That's a shame."

She crossed her arms over her chest and looked at him. "Why?"

"Because most of the time the person doing the helping benefits more than the one being helped."

"I don't understand."

"It feels good to help someone."

"Then the motivation is to make yourself feel good?" she said.

"No, that's a side benefit," he said, turning onto the ranch's long drive. "You help people because, well, you want to."

"I'm not following the logic."

"Logic is up here." He pointed to his head. "What I'm talking about lives here." He placed an open palm against his chest.

She didn't respond—she couldn't. There was something so real about this man, real and vulnerable. She couldn't remember the last time she'd allowed herself to be vulnerable.

"Let's table the philosophy discussion for another time," he said, parking in front of the main house.

She nodded and opened her door, a bit anxious about how she'd be received by the family. Would they consider her a burden, like she'd been to her own family? Voices of the past taunted her, mocked her. Why was she thinking about the past?

Sleep and recovery. That's what she needed.

She hoped the family would be asleep so Brie wouldn't have to be social or charming or any of those things that most people were naturally good at but that took a lot of energy for her to accomplish.

As they approached the front door, Jacob offered a smile. "It'll be fine."

Again, he was promising something he couldn't know for certain, which was why she found it hard to trust him.

"Ready?" he said.

She nodded. He swung open the door, and a black dog charged them.

"Oscar, halt!" a woman cried.

The animal skidded to a stop a few inches from Brie and Jacob, its tail swishing against the floor in a frantic wag. Dogs weren't her thing, and they usually sensed it.

"Right here," a young woman, about Brie's age, said from the kitchen. The dog begrudgingly went to its master's side and lay down with a harrumph.

"Sorry about that," the woman said.

Lacey stood next to her, drinking tea.

"That's why your father doesn't like him in the house," Lacey said.

"He's a good watchdog," she countered.

The dog whined, his gaze focused on Jacob.

"We haven't met." The young woman approached Brie and offered her hand. "I'm Rose Rogers, Lacey and Bill's daughter."

"Nice to meet you," Brie said.

"So, you're the celebrity, huh?" Rose went back to the kitchen.

"Celebrity?"

"The woman who fell into the river, is being stalked by bad guys and is hiding out at Boulder Creek Ranch."

"I didn't choose to come back here."

The women shot each other a look. Brie suspected her comment sounded abrupt, maybe even rude.

"What she meant was, bringing her here was my idea," Jacob said. "Rose, release Oscar."

"You sure?"

He motioned with his hands. The dog's tail thumped on the floor.

"Oscar…" The dog looked up at Rose. "Release."

He charged Jacob and practically jumped into his arms. "You're a good boy, Oscar. Don't let them tell you different."

"Yeah, and you're a softie," Lacey said.

"I didn't think anyone would be up," Jacob said, petting the dog.

"I finished a search-and-rescue training nearby and texted to see if Mom was up," Rose said.

"I'm always up for you, honey." Lacey put her arm around Rose and gave her a squeeze.

Brie had to look away, that childhood ache igniting in her chest. Her eyes connected with the dog's eyes. As if he sensed her melancholy, he broke free of Jacob, walked over and sat on Brie's foot, looking up over his shoulder at her.

"What does he want?" Brie said.

"Pet him," Jacob suggested.

She tentatively reached down and tapped his head a few times. "I… I'm sorry, I don't do dogs."

"I don't blame you," Lacey said. "They're stinky and demanding and—"

"Don't listen to her, Oscar," Rose countered.

"You don't have to *do* anything," Jacob said to Brie. "Well, except love him."

"He'll give it back tenfold and then some," Rose said.

As Oscar watched Brie with his wide brown eyes, she could almost see the love there.

She really did need a good night's sleep. Understanding and appreciating a dog's behavior and taking help from strangers was not like her. Then again, brain trauma could affect a person's temperament and personality.

She withdrew her hand from the dog's soft fur, but he didn't move off her foot.

"Mrs. Rogers—"

"Mrs. Rogers is my mother-in-law," Lacey interrupted Brie. "Call me Lacey."

"Lacey, I'd like to thank you for allowing me to stay at the ranch. I will leave as soon as I am able."

"Good luck with that," Rose teased.

As Brie puzzled over Rose's comment, Lacey crossed the room and took Brie's hand. "You may stay as long as necessary."

"I don't want to be a burden."

"You won't be. We're all about service to others." With a nod she let go and went back to drinking her tea at the kitchen island. "Besides, we could use an extra hand around here."

"Let's give her a few days to recover," Jacob said. "And for the record, her name is Sara Clark."

"Ooh, an alias," Rose said, her eyes widening.

"I won't need a few days," Brie said.

"Brianna—"

"Sara," Brianna corrected Jacob. "I won't feel like I'm taking advantage of your generous nature if I'm helping out. I will work for you, but right now I need to sleep."

"Okay, then," Rose said.

"I'm sorry, was that too abrupt?" Brianna said. "I don't have the best social skills. I apologize in advance if I accidentally offend anyone."

"Your self-awareness is impressive," Jacob countered. "I'll show you to your living quarters." He glanced at Lacey. "The Alpine Cabin?"

Lacey nodded. "It's ready to go with fresh linens and toiletries. Jacob is right—you should take a day or two to recover."

"Thank you."

Jacob escorted Brianna across the compound to one of the seven free-standing cabins they usually reserved for family or friends. Thankfully it was vacant, clean and ready for whoever happened to drop by. Lacey and Bill had a large family back east that liked to visit. Jacob appreciated how they kept this cabin available for visitors.

He unlocked the door and flipped on the lights. Brianna's eyes widened.

"What's wrong? Too small?" he said.

"No, it's very…rustic."

"Yeah, took me a while to get used to things out West, too."

"It's a real log cabin?" She touched the wood wall.

"Yep, authentic Douglas fir."

"It's good strategy, housing me far away from everyone."

"Wait, that's not why we set you up here. The lodge rooms and other cabins are booked. Plus, I thought you'd like your own space. Living in the main house with everyone can get a little… overwhelming."

"Do you live there?"

"Yes. I want to be near Miri, and she likes to be close to her grandparents."

Brie wandered through the room, running her hands along the wooden dresser.

"I can take you into town tomorrow for a phone, probably around ten if that works. I'll get someone to cover the trail ride for me."

"Trail ride?"

"We take guests on any number of rides in the morning and again in the afternoon."

"Thanks. I'll need clothes, too."

"Right, wrangler clothes."

She cocked her head.

"Jeans, cowboy boots, a cowboy hat," he clarified. "In the meantime, you'll find toiletries in the bathroom—oh, and this—" He opened a dresser drawer and pulled out a few items of clothing. "Nightshirt, sweats, sweatshirt. To get you through tonight. The thermostat is over there." He pointed to the dial on the wall. "It can drop to thirty this time of year. Is this your first time to Montana?"

"Yes."

He suddenly felt silly talking about the weather and asking inane questions. "Anyway, feel free to make yourself coffee in the morning and relax on the porch before breakfast. Lacey will ring the bell half an hour before we serve a hot breakfast in the house. You'll hear us bringing the horses in from the pasture for the trail rides. It's a great sound. There are a lot of great things about this part of the country."

She nodded, hugging herself. He wished he knew the right thing to say to make her feel safe.

"Lacey and Bill had a staff meeting earlier explaining your situation, with orders to keep an eye out for anything suspicious and to make sure you have everything you need. We've got over a dozen staff members who all know how to ride and shoot."

"If the employees know about me, won't word get out that I'm here?"

"We're family, Brianna. We protect our own."

"But I'm not a member of this family."

"You are now."

* * *

Brianna awakened the next morning to sunshine streaming through a crack in the curtain. She could hardly believe she'd slept considering all that had happened to her yesterday. But once she climbed under the covers, it hadn't taken long to drift off, and she was grateful for the peaceful seven-plus hours of slumber.

She awoke with a slight headache—no surprise there. She wrapped herself in the thick robe, wanting some fresh air to clear her mind. Back in Chicago, stepping out on her condo balcony with a cup of coffee always helped wake her up. Today she opened the cabin door and froze at the breathtaking beauty before her. Back home she'd be assaulted by city sounds—horns, car engines, various construction clatter—whereas right now the most dominant noise was...

A rhythmic clap. She glanced right and saw a dozen horses being led past the cabins toward the main house and corral.

She wasn't an animal person per se, but even Brianna couldn't rip her gaze from the strong and majestic creatures as they trotted down the dirt road.

She took a step onto the porch and kicked something. So enthralled by the horses, she didn't notice a thermos and cooler right in front of her. A note read, "Coffee & breakfast. Find me when you're up. Jacob."

Opening the cooler, she pulled out a plate covered in plastic wrap with muffins, scones and sweet rolls. She took the food and coffee into her cabin, set it on the small table and stepped back. She couldn't remember the last time someone had been thoughtful enough to bring her morning coffee.

"You're his project," she said. "He's being a Good Samaritan, earning points with God. That's all."

Yet his gesture made her ache for something she couldn't quite name.

"It's the head injury," she whispered, fighting back the strange emotions bubbling up in her chest.

Brianna was a strong, independent woman dedicated to her research and destined to live alone. She'd accepted her fate early in life, and no threat, danger or even caring gestures from a man like Jacob would change that.

She knew who she was, what she was about.

A soft tap at the door jarred her out of her thoughts. She went to the door and peered through a peephole. It was Rose from last night.

Brianna opened the door. Oscar the dog sat beside Rose.

"Good morning," Rose said. "You got the coffee and pastries?"

"I did, thank you."

She handed her a plastic bag. "Some extra clothes until you go shopping. I guessed on your size. Sorry, it's all Boulder Creek Guest Ranch stuff, sweatshirt and staff jacket —oh, and a spare set of cowboy boots until you get your own."

Brianna peeked in the bag. "Thank you."

"Jacob wanted me to tell you he's in the barn. Come down whenever you're ready. He's doing chores until he takes you to town."

"I hate interrupting his day."

"Not a problem. He got his trail ride covered, so he's clear until the campfire tonight."

"What about his daughter?"

"Miri hangs out in Little Wrangler's Club during the day. How are you feeling? How's the concussion? I've had my share of those."

Brie frowned in question.

"Falling off horses. I didn't get the cowboy gene." She shrugged. "But I'm good with other animals, right, Oscar?" He thumped his tail against the wooden porch.

"I don't suppose you'd want to take me into town?" Brie said.

"What, did you and Jacob have a fight already? You haven't even known each other twenty-four hours."

"I feel like I've put him out so much—the river, the hospital, convincing your family to let me stay here."

"It didn't take much convincing. We all voted, including the staff. They are, after all, our extended family."

"You voted to let me stay and potentially bring danger to the ranch?"

"Well, I heard the danger is one guy and the cops have a description of him."

"Actually, there were two other men—"

"So, three guys to our twenty-plus. We're not worried. Besides, they'd have to find you first and would probably never guess you'd stay at a ranch, right?"

"How did you…?"

"I researched you online—your work, education, social media. You're highly educated and respected in your field. Finding alternatives to healing autoimmune disease, right? Sounds like noble work. I'm guessing you've never been on a horse or stepped foot into a barn."

"Correct."

"Then the ranch is a good place to hide."

With a smile, Rose turned and made a *chick-chick* sound that was some kind of code for the dog. As she walked away, Oscar trotted obediently beside her.

Brianna felt like she'd stepped into a foreign world where strangers offered unconditional support without expecting anything in return.

It didn't make sense, and it made her nervous.

* * *

Jacob was showing a ten-year-old guest named Adam how to brush down Teddy, an Appaloosa, when he saw Brianna enter the barn.

"Sara," he greeted.

"Hello, Jacob."

She looked better today, although she still limped. "We should get you crutches."

"Not necessary." She straightened.

It was like she didn't want to appear weak, yet Jacob knew what she'd been through, so this act of strength must be for others' benefit.

"You ready to go?" Jacob asked.

She nodded. "Yes, thank you."

"Rick," Jacob called a teenager over. "Can you help Adam finish brushing down Teddy?"

"Sure." The teenager passed by Brie and said, "Good morning, Sara."

"Good morning."

"We'll be back in a few hours," Jacob said.

He motioned Brie out of the barn toward his truck.

"I feel bad taking you away from your work."

"It's fine. The family gave me a list of things to pick up." He flashed the piece of paper with requests and tucked it into his jacket pocket. "They'll probably text me another dozen things before we get to town."

"Really?"

"It's not like in the city, where you can get to Target in ten minutes. It'll take a good forty minutes to get to the general store. That's eighty minutes travel time, plus however long it takes to shop, so a trip to town is kind of a big deal— has to be planned into the workday."

"I'll be quick."

"I wasn't saying that to rush you. Me going to town is an opportunity for others to benefit. It's hard to schedule time off for staff members during the high season."

"They work seven days a week?"

"Work," he chuckled. "Yeah, I guess you could call it that."

He opened the door to his truck.

"What would you call it?"

"When you love what you do, it doesn't really feel like work."

She climbed into his truck, and he shut the door. Someone like Brianna probably couldn't understand the wrangler mentality. Jacob surely didn't when he'd first moved out here. It took him a few months to appreciate the completely different kind of lifestyle those at the Boulder Creek Ranch enjoyed, and why some of them had given up high-intensity careers for life at the ranch.

Brianna wasn't into small talk, and Jacob didn't want to push her on more important issues, like if she remembered more about her attempted kidnappings, so it was a quiet ride to the supply store.

They made good time picking out what she needed. Brianna wanted to purchase her items, but to avoid anyone tracking her credit card, he offered to pay for everything with the ranch's card and she could reimburse them.

He asked her to stay close while he picked out the rest of the requests from friends at the ranch. She seemed to limp less when she leaned on the shopping cart, so he let her guide it up and down the aisles.

As they approached the register to check out, Deidre Wilson sidled toward them.

"Jacob," she greeted.

"Hello, Deidre," he said.

Deidre eyed Brianna, then smiled at Jacob. "Who's this?"

"Sara Clark, a new wrangler at Boulder Creek."

"Oh." Deidre's tense smile eased a bit.

Rumors swirled that Deidre was in the market for a husband, and Jacob's name was near the top of that list. But he had no interest in romance or marriage. His priority was, and always would be, Miri.

"We've gotta get back," he said. "I'll tell Lacey and Bill you said hi." Jacob continued to scan items in the self-check lane.

"Good to see you, Jacob," Deidre said.

"Yeah, have a good day."

Out of the corner of his eye, he spotted her walk away, and his shoulders relaxed. It was important to convince folks in town that Brianna was a new employee, not a scientist hiding out from a mysterious threat.

"What was that about?" Brianna asked.

"Deidre's a friend of the family."

"You sure that's all?" She raised an eyebrow.

"Don't you start."

With a slight smile, she handed him a package of undershirts for Miri, and their hands touched. He tried not letting the connection disturb his focus, but it definitely threw him off.

Understandable. He and Brianna had an unusual closeness due to the intense experiences they'd shared in the last twenty-some hours. She handed him men's socks that were on his list for Rick.

"Oh, I forgot socks for me," she said. "I know where they are. I'll be right back."

"Brie—Sara, wait."

She waved him off and disappeared from sight around a corner. He kicked into overdrive, wanting to wrap up this shopping trip and get back to the ranch, where he knew she'd be safe. What was she thinking taking off like that?

Whoa, she's not your kid. She's a grown woman.

A beautiful woman. He shoved the thought aside. Totally inappropriate.

A few minutes later Brianna still wasn't back, and a line was forming behind him. He finished paying, grabbed the receipt and went to find her.

He turned the corner to the women's socks aisle.

No Brianna. He went down another aisle, and a third. "Sara?" he called out.

His heart pounded in his chest.

Deidre poked her head around a corner, "If you're looking for your new wrangler, she left out the back with two handsome men."

SIX

Brianna felt she had no choice but to accompany the two men from yesterday's attack toward a black Suburban. She wanted to draw them away from the store, from Jacob.

She would not risk him getting hurt trying to save her.

She would not risk a little girl losing her father.

"We're here to protect you, not hurt you," Eric said.

Sure, and she was Madame Curie.

"Where are you taking me?" she asked.

"Missoula," the man named Eric said.

"Why?"

"Our boss needs to speak with you, to explain things," Eric said.

"What things?"

"Above my pay grade."

The other man, who she assumed was Eric's partner, Bobby, had walked ahead of them and opened the back door of the Suburban.

Statistically speaking, a kidnapping victim's survival rate decreased dramatically once she got into the kidnapper's car. But how could she avoid it? It was Brianna against two burly men. As her mind raced with possible solutions, the acute sound of the store's fire alarm blared across the parking lot. The momentary distraction gave her the chance to fight back. She kicked Eric in the shin and took off, hobbling away from them.

She didn't turn around, didn't bother to see how close he was to grabbing her and tossing her in the back of the vehicle.

Then she saw Jacob sprint from the store wielding a shovel.

"Sara!" he called out.

"Jacob," she uttered.

He was closing in.

She feared her kidnappers were closer.

Instead of feeling Eric grab her, she heard tires squeal against the pavement.

She stumbled and hit the ground, gasping for air. Suddenly Jacob was there, next to her.

"Are you hurt?" he said.

"Those men…"

"They're gone."

She looked over her shoulder and spotted the SUV speeding away.

"Let's get you back to the ranch." He helped her stand and guided her to the truck. "Back seat this time. Those windows are tinted. Keep your head down."

"Where are you going?"

"To get our stuff. Lock the doors and don't let anyone in."

She didn't respond right away, still trying to calm the surge of adrenaline.

"Brianna? Dr. Wilkes?"

She looked at him. He gently touched her chin with his forefinger. "It really is okay. For the moment, anyway. I'll be right back."

She nodded, and he shut the door.

They reported the kidnapping attempt to Detective Harper and hurried back to the ranch for Brianna's safety.

No one knew she'd taken up residence there.

She hoped.

When they pulled onto the ranch property, she saw guests in the distance sitting around picnic tables, eating, chatting and laughing.

Such a normal scene in contrast to what Brianna had just experienced.

"I can drop you at your cabin to chill out if you want," Jacob said.

"What about you?"

"I need to help with lunch unless…you need me?"

She nearly responded that she didn't need anyone but caught herself. Brianna would be at the mercy of those men if he hadn't helped her today.

"Thank you, but I'm better now. My heart rate has dropped to sixty beats per minute, and my breathing is back to normal."

"Well, that's good to hear."

"Are you teasing me?"

"No, not at all. I'm glad you're so attuned to your physical condition. Not many people are."

"Mentally speaking, I'd like to keep busy. Resting in my cabin will give my mind an opportunity to drift to dark places."

"Makes sense. You want to help with lunch or brush the horses?"

"Lunch."

He pulled into a parking spot. "We'll unpack the supplies later. Let's see where they're at with lunch."

As he reached for his door handle, she touched his arm. "Jacob?"

"Yes, ma'am?" He looked at her with those warm green eyes.

"Did you tell anyone what happened?"

"At the ranch? Not yet, why?"

"Once you do, I am prepared to relocate."

"I doubt the Rogers clan will let you leave until they know you're safe."

"My being here is risking their safety."

"Stop thinking that way. No one followed us."

"How did they find me at the store?"

"It's the only store within a hundred miles where you can get everything you need in one place. Sooner or later you'd have to stop here to get necessities, and they were waiting. As simple as that. Plus, they have no idea what car you drove off in, because they fled the scene before us."

"But they saw you."

"Yeah, me and my great big shovel," he joked.

"Rose said everyone here knows how to shoot, yet you don't carry a gun?"

"No, I don't. And I never will. Let's help with lunch."

Jacob got out of the truck and went around to open Brianna's door. He wanted to forget his knee-jerk reaction to her gun question. He'd been out West a year and still couldn't get used to the idea of carrying a firearm. It might be a part of the culture here, and necessary for wildlife threats, but he'd experienced too much tragedy from gun abuse in the city and couldn't bear the thought of handling one, much less using it on something or someone.

Brianna was already out of the truck by the time he reached her door.

"I think we should tell Lacey and Bill what happened," she said.

"We will, but—"

"If I need to leave, I'd like to do it sooner than later."

Her cheeks were flushed, and her lips pursed into a thin line. He suspected that sixty-beats-per-minute number had spiked. The signs were obvious: she was stressing out about her fate at the ranch, and he had to convince her she had nothing to worry about.

"Tell you what, you go inside to the den and I'll bring Lacey and Bill in for a quick conference, okay?"

"That would be ideal."

As he walked her to the front door, Lacey came out to greet them. "Oh, good, you're back. We could use the extra hands in the kitchen."

"We need to talk to you about something," Jacob said.

"After lunch." Lacey motioned them inside.

Brianna didn't move. "Two men tried to kidnap me in town."

Lacey looked at Jacob, then back at Brianna. A few tense seconds passed, and Jacob could almost feel the anxiety drifting off Brianna as she stood beside him.

"Oh, honey." Lacey reached out and gave Brianna a hug. "That must have been terrifying."

Jacob stepped around them and noticed Brianna's shocked expression. This was not the reaction she'd expected.

"I... I understand if you want me to find other lodging," Brianna said.

Lacey broke the embrace. "Stop that talk and come help with lunch, but only if you're up to it."

"I am, but I can't cook."

"Nonsense, everyone can cook. Besides, I hear you're a smart lady. You can learn anything if you put your mind to it, right?"

"Most things, I suspect."

Lacey interlaced her arm in Brianna's and escorted her into the house.

Jacob took one more look around the property. He'd been keeping up a strong front, but truth was, the random kidnapping attempt made him a little paranoid as well.

"She's cute," Rose said, joining him on the porch. Oscar the dog glanced up at her. "Go ahead."

The dog rushed Jacob. He knelt to pet him. "Wait, what?"

"Brianna. She's cute, in an intellectual sort of way."

"She's complicated," he muttered.

"You wouldn't want boring."

"She's a researcher from Chicago. She'll be gone in a few days."

"Maybe."

"What are you up to?" he said.

She shrugged. "I want Miri's dad to be happy. Someone in this family should be happy."

"Hey, your parents are blissfully happy."

"They're the exception to most rules of relationships."

"When did you become so cynical?"

"I guess big brother is rubbing off on me."

"Is Beau out back with the guests? I need to tell him about what happened today."

"What happened?"

"Two guys tried to kidnap Brianna."

"Yikes. Did you notify T.J. yet?"

"T.J.?" He winked. "You mean Detective Harper. Yes, we called him on the way back to the ranch."

"You think he'll come to interview her?" she said with hope in her voice.

"When are you two gonna grab a coffee and see if something sparks?"

"When he stops blaming himself for Cassie's death." She snapped her gaze to Jacob. "Sorry, sorry, I didn't mean to bring it up. I—"

"Rose, don't apologize. We agreed to keep talking about Cassie so Miri would remember her mom."

"I know, but I still feel horrible that you didn't even know you had a daughter until Cassie had passed away."

Jacob stood, and the dog looked up at him, begging for more attention.

"I don't get why Detective Harper feels responsible," Jacob said.

"Cassie was supposed to be with T.J. that night, not hanging out at Silverdale Pub with Brad Martin."

"T.J. and Cassie were dating?"

"Maybe? Or thinking about it. Anyway, he feels guilty about blowing her off and not making a strong enough case against Martin years ago to put him behind bars."

Jacob shook his head.

"What?"

"So much guilt. I pray that at some point we're all able to stop beating ourselves up about the poor choices my ex-fiancée made that left her child without a mother."

The borderline cruel words left a bitter taste in his mouth. Ashamed by the outburst, he turned abruptly and found himself looking at Brianna. She must have overheard the exchange.

"I need you. I mean, we need you in the kitchen," Brianna said.

He glanced at Rose. "I'm sorry."

"What for? Speaking the truth?"

He entered the house, still berating himself for the harsh words. Rose said he spoke the truth. That might very well be, but it was uncalled for, unnecessary to speak ill of Miri's mom.

"You're upset," Brianna said.

"I'm fine."

"I can tell you're not fine by the pulse in your neck and the color of your cheeks."

"Can't hide anything from you, can I?"

"You're joking again, which means you're uncomfortable."

"I don't always joke when I'm uncomfortable," he said as they entered the kitchen. "What do you need help with?"

"Could you finish cutting the desserts and put them on plates? I want to call my lab and let them know I'm okay."

"Sure."

"I'll be right back to help serve."

"Don't give anyone your location."

"I'm calling my research partner, and the foundation that supports our project."

"I understand, but their phones might be tapped. Use the cell phone we bought you, not the house landline. Have you got your cell phone?"

She pulled it out of her back pocket and held it up, seemingly irritated.

"I'm only trying to protect you," he said.

"I appreciate that. I'll be right back."

Brianna disappeared around the corner. She needed privacy, he understood that, but he wished she would've have stayed in the kitchen where he could keep an eye on her.

After washing his hands, he put on gloves and grabbed a knife. As he started cutting the brownies, he wondered if Brianna's decision-making skills would improve as the concussion subsided. Because leaving him to find socks at the store hadn't been a smart move, and she didn't seem concerned about sharing her location with people at her lab.

She was an intelligent woman, yet the trauma of the past twenty-four hours had thrown her off her game. Jacob knew the feeling. He'd been thrown off plenty in his life but was able to recover with the help of friends and faith, two things she had made clear were missing in her life.

"Then it's a good thing she's here," he said softly to himself and sliced the brownies.

"I'm a little shaken, Douglas. But I'll be fine," Brianna said to her research partner as she stepped into the den. She didn't want him worrying about her. It would distract him from their current project.

"You're not telling me something. I hear it in your voice," Douglas said.

"I was injured in the mountains because someone's after me."

Silence.

"Douglas?"

"After you, as in…?"

"Men have tried to kidnap me. Multiple times."

"I am so sorry, Brianna. Are you in danger? Where are you now?"

"Staying outside of town with a friend. I'm

safe for the moment and plan to head home in a few days."

"The board chairman called twice today to speak with you. He said you're not answering your phone."

"I lost it in the mountains. I'm calling you from a new, prepaid phone."

"Are they after our research?"

"I'm honestly not sure."

"I'm worried about you, your safety."

This morning Brianna would have also been worried, but every time she found herself in danger, a protector appeared— a protector by the name of Jacob Rush.

"Thank you, Douglas. I appreciate your concern, but truly, I'm safe."

At least for the time being.

"Will you be back for the board meeting Friday?"

"Ah, the board meeting. We should probably reschedule." In truth, she didn't remember scheduling that meeting.

"You promised results from the latest controlled studies."

"I did? But we haven't completed analyzing the data."

Silence.

"Douglas?"

"We completed it last week."

She leaned against a wooden desk, a flurry of panic shattering her thoughts.

"That's right," she said, covering her trepidation.

Get a hold of yourself. She had to act as if she was fine, as if she wasn't forgetting things, teetering on the precipice of losing her career, her future.

"Let's push the board meeting off a full week. I should be able to travel by next Monday and will return to the lab."

"If your motel was broken into, what happened to your laptop?"

"I'm not sure I brought it with me."

"Not sure? Brianna, that laptop has critical data on it."

"I'm aware of that, Douglas." She didn't appreciate his tone, even if she understood his concern.

"I'm worried about you. Have you seen a doctor?"

"Yes. Sprained ankle, bruised ribs and concussion."

"The concussion explains the cognitive deficiencies."

She clenched her jaw, afraid of what might come out of her mouth.

"Are you taking anything for the pain? An anti-inflammatory? That might help the swelling of the brain as well."

"Yes, I have what I need." She was starting to feel like a child being told how to take care of herself.

"Good, good. Please be careful, Brianna. And check in daily. I feel better when I know you're okay."

"Thank you. I will touch base tomorrow."

"You might want to give Viceroy a call."

"I will."

"I won't tell anyone about your condition or where you are."

"That would be great."

"Stay safe."

"I will."

She ended the call and gazed out the window. Guests and wranglers sat at four long tables eating, drinking and enjoying conversation. They hadn't a care in the world, their expressions so opposite the worry weaving its way through Brianna's body.

She didn't remember things, important things like having finished analyzing data and calling a board meeting to share her findings. How was that possible? Forgetting things that had happened right before a traumatic event was typical, but forgetting selective things from the recent past? That didn't seem right.

Unless…a part of her wanted to forget. But why? Because then her project would be completed? She'd have spent most of her adult life working on a protocol to ease symptoms of debilitating autoimmune diseases, and once she'd accomplished her goal, she would do what, exactly?

Because there wasn't another disease as important or close to her heart as the one that took her little sister's life and essentially destroyed Brie's family.

Another scenario flooded to the surface, one where she realized she hadn't proven her theory and had wasted the last eight years of her life and millions of dollars.

She had failed.

Her heart rate sped up, and her aunt's voice echoed in her mind.

A silly girl.

A worthless, stupid girl.

Brianna bit back a gasp. She thought she'd fully eradicated those memories, buried them in a place where they wouldn't taunt her anymore. It served no purpose to remember the cruelty. It would only destabilize her thoughts and emotions.

"Guests are getting restless for chocolate," Jacob said from the den doorway.

When she didn't respond, he approached her and frowned.

"Whoa, who died?" he said.

"My sister, my mother," she blurted out.

"Oh, Brianna, I'm so sorry."

She could tell he wanted to comfort her with a hug. Oddly, she would have welcomed it.

"Like today or...?" he pushed.

"No, when I was ten and thirteen years old." She sighed. "I remember that day with such clarity," she started. "The day they told us Abigail had passed—what I was wearing, what I'd eaten for lunch—and then three years later when the police officers came to the house and told my father my mother had crashed her car into a tree." She glanced at Jacob. "I made my father meat loaf and peas for dinner."

Jacob offered a sympathetic expression.

"That was nearly twenty years ago, and I remember it so well. Yet I can't remember an upcoming critical board meeting where I am supposed to present the final results of our research. It's like pieces of the past few months have been wiped from my brain."

"It will come back. Give it time."

"I don't have time!" she said in a raised voice.

Someone shut the door to the den, probably so Brianna's outburst wouldn't alarm guests.

She sighed. "They don't have time."

"The people who will benefit from your research?"

"Yes."

"This stress is probably not helping your condition."

She half chuckled.

"I said something funny?"

"No, it's just, stress is one of the factors we used in our controlled studies."

"See, you remembered that. The rest will come back to you."

She fought back tears. "What if it doesn't?"

"Have faith."

"But—"

"It's an expression, Brianna. You don't have to believe in God to have faith in a positive outcome."

"You believe in God."

"Yes."

"Why would your God bring me to this point, so close to helping people, and then slam the door in my face?"

"I could spout any number of clichés, like when God closes a door, He opens a window. But the reality, at least for me, is that faith sees us through our trials. Faith, and surrender to a higher power."

"I wish I could surrender all this consternation."

"You can. First, you have to breathe." He took a breath in and out with her. "Now repeat after me—I cast my worries upon the Lord, and I go free."

"But I don't believe in your Lord."

"You said stress was something you were researching?"

"Yes."

"And anxiety causes stress, right?"

She nodded.

"I'm assuming your work focused on ways to reduce anxiety?"

"That is correct."

"Like…?"

"Breath work, meditation—"

"Think of meditation like prayer. Prayer is a form of surrendering your stress. By casting your worries to the Lord, you're basically handing it to Him to carry for you so you can rest and recover. See how that works?"

She nodded. "I don't feel worthy of asking Him for help, since I don't worship Him."

"God loves all His children." Jacob took her hands, inhaled deeply and nodded.

"I cast my worry upon the Lord, and I go free," she said along with him. For the briefest of moments, Brianna felt the heaviness in her chest ease. Her heart rate slowed; her panicked thoughts quieted.

"Better?" he said.

"Actually, yes."

"Good." He squeezed her hands gently and released them. "Let's go serve dessert."

As the lunch progressed, Brianna seemed better. Jacob even caught her smiling from time to time. She opted out of the afternoon trail ride and retreated to her cabin, so he checked in with her before he accompanied guests up Majestic Mountain. He didn't like leaving Brianna alone, but knew the Boulder Creek Ranch family would keep an eye on her.

Family. He'd never known what he was missing until God brought him out here to join the Rogers clan. Jacob's own father had been obsessed with work, and his mother was busy with her job as an activist, which took up most of her time. Jacob and his sister, Beth, were pretty much on their own by the time they reached adolescence. He thought all kids were independent at age thirteen.

On some level he suspected he was missing out, and was afraid of failing as a parent, because having his own kids had never been in his plan. No, he'd devoted all his time, energy and passion into developing a program designed to help police officers with nonemergency calls.

As he led the guests on horseback back down the mountain to the ranch, Jacob scanned the horizon. It seemed a lifetime ago that he'd gone on calls with Curt. Jacob had proven to the Detroit PD the value of having social workers offer their expertise in situations like attempted suicide or domestic altercations. He and Curt had experienced some successes, but also some failures.

Like Kara Roberts. The teenager's death had

eaten away at Jacob, making him question his purpose on this earth.

His angry speech about not bringing children into this violent world must have terrified Cassie. It was only a week later that she'd broken their engagement and left, a crushing blow that caused him to withdraw even further into the darkness. Then Pastor Williams showed up at Jacob's apartment and challenged him to see the truth: Jacob was being entitled and disrespectful if he continued to wallow in self-pity in the name of Kara Roberts's death. Pastor Williams challenged Jacob to find his faith, to follow the Lord's directives and do good in the world.

After much prayer and some healing, Jacob went back to work. He focused on maintaining strong boundaries so the job wouldn't eat away at him. Some days he was successful, other days not so much.

Four years later, Lacey and Bill's attorney had contacted him, notifying Jacob he had a child.

The world as he knew it seemed to flip upside down. Shame, guilt, regret all wrestled for control, to which his pastor recommended he surrender his burden to God and follow His lead.

Jacob hadn't regretted a single moment of taking that advice.

He helped bring the horses into the barn to remove saddles and brush them down before taking them out to pasture for the night.

As he loosened the cinch on Sarge, he thanked God for leading him out West. He'd never really felt a part of a family until he joined the Boulder Creek Ranch family. There were times when he sensed Lacey and Bill were unsure about Jacob's parenting skills, but in the end they all wanted the same thing: for Miri to be a happy, healthy and well-adjusted child.

"Are you okay?"

He turned and found Brianna standing there, studying him. "Hey, how are you feeling? Did you rest? Keep the ankle elevated?"

"I did. You didn't answer my question."

"I'm fine, why?"

"Your expression seemed…"

"I was thinking. Dangerous, I know." He smiled.

She returned his smile, and his breath caught. He snapped his attention back to the cinch. He didn't want to get confused about things, confused about his role in Dr. Wilkes's life. He was helping her out, but it was nothing more than that. It couldn't be anything more than that. She had a career back in Chicago, and he was committed to his new family in a wonderful part of the country.

"I called the foundation, and they still want me to have bodyguards."

He glanced at her.

"I declined. I hope that doesn't put my work in jeopardy."

"I don't see why it would." He removed the saddle, and she approached with a brush.

"From their point of view, I'm suffering from a concussion, which could cause me to make poor choices." She looked at him. "Brain trauma can do that to a person."

"Yes, I know." He picked up a brush and joined her in grooming Sarge. "You're doing a good job there." He nodded at her hand, working in a circular motion.

"I went online in the den and viewed videos on how to do this."

"Ah."

"Papa Jay!" Miri said, racing into the barn.

"Hey, tiger." He picked her up and gave her a squeeze. She giggled, filling his heart with joy.

"I'm not a tiger, I'm an owl!" She waved her owl in his face.

"Well then, Miss Owl—"

"No, not a miss! Just Owl!"

"Okay, Owl, what've you been up to?"

"Made more pine-cone owls in Little Wrangler's Club, and I made baby owl a bed with covers made of tissue."

"You're amazing." He kissed her cheek.

"I want to go find a real owl." She looked at Brianna. "Have you ever seen one?"

"I have not."

"Then you should come, too."

"How will you find them? They tend to blend in with their environment," Brie said.

"What's vry-ment?"

"The woods, the trees," Jacob said.

"You could bring a flashlight, unless you think that would scare them," Brie offered.

"Nothing scares an owl," Miri said proudly.

"Maybe tomorrow," Jacob said.

"What about now?" Miri protested.

"I've got chores, then dinner. Doesn't Nanna need your help making biscuits for dinner?"

"Work, work, work. There's always work to do. I want to go owl hunting."

"We will, honey, promise," Jacob said.

She squirmed out of his arms and dashed off.

"If I had half her energy…" Jacob said with a slight chuckle.

"She's a lucky little girl to have you as her father."

"Thanks, but I'm the one who's blessed."

Jacob was pleasantly surprised that Brie helped with the horses until it was time for dinner prep. It seemed like she didn't stray far from Jacob, and he wondered if that was for her benefit or his. She'd obviously sensed his melancholy mood this afternoon, and he hadn't answered her direct question: *Are you okay?*

His answer would be too complicated to share in a few minutes, or even an hour. Some days he was okay, other days he struggled. Those were the days when he'd be yanked into the darker corners of his past, reminded how he had failed others. Then he'd pray for forgiveness and feel a little better.

Most days he was able to stay present and savored his role as father and brother, and perhaps even son to Lacey and Bill. He didn't seek validation from them, exactly, but it made him feel good to lighten their burden, both physically and emotionally. He sensed on some level they feared he'd want to move away with Miri, and he tried whenever appropriate to ease their concern.

He pulled rolls out of the oven and dumped them into towel-lined wicker baskets. He glanced across the kitchen at Brianna, who scooped beef stew into flanged soup bowls, measuring precisely to make them equal. She eyed the freshly chopped parsley on the cutting board and frowned.

"What?" he said.

"The instructions are to sprinkle parsley on top. How much is a sprinkle? I'd better check the internet."

She started for the door.

"Hang on, you don't need to look it up."

"I don't want to ruin the meal."

"Sometimes you have to use your instinct."

Her brows knit together.

"Here." He pinched some parsley between his

fingers and dropped it over a serving of stew. "How does that look?"

"How is it supposed to look?"

"Appetizing, I guess. It's mostly for decoration. No one taught you to cook?"

"Not really, although I could make a few practiced favorites." She imitated his move and sprinkled parsley on another bowl of stew.

Wrangler Heidi entered the kitchen. "This tray ready?" she asked.

"One moment, please." Brianna finished sprinkling parsley on the six bowls and nodded at Heidi.

"Thanks," Heidi said, carrying the tray out of the kitchen.

Brianna carefully filled six more bowls with stew and placed them on a second tray.

Wrangler Chip popped his head into the kitchen. "Rolls and butter?"

Jacob handed him two roll baskets complete with cups of individual butters. Brianna sprinkled more parsley on the stew and looked at Jacob for approval.

"Like a pro," he said. "A professional parsley sprinkler."

"You're making fun of me."

"No, I'm not. Brianna, sometimes people tease because they're trying to make you smile. They aren't judging you. They don't have a sinister motive."

"That has not been my experience."

"I'm sorry to hear that. Laughter is important, at least to me."

Rose stepped into the doorway. "Have you guys seen Oscar?"

Lacey passed Rose and headed for the sink with an empty water pitcher in her hand. "What's that rascal up to now?"

"I put him in the den to chill, but the door's open and I can't find him."

"He's probably hiding under the table hoping some softie will give him a bite of Mom's buttermilk biscuit," Jacob said, and caught himself. He'd called Lacey *Mom.*

Rose raised an eyebrow, Brianna studied Jacob and Lacey stood with her back to him, filling the pitcher at the sink.

"Uh, sorry. Lacey," he said.

Lacey turned and offered a genuine smile. "Don't be. I'm honored that you'd call me Mom." Still smiling, she carried the water pitcher into the dining room.

"I've gotta find Oscar before he swipes somebody's stew." Rose disappeared from the kitchen.

"Well, that was awkward," he muttered.

"She didn't seem upset, did she?"

"I don't know. She can be hard to read sometimes."

A few minutes later Jacob and Brianna joined

the group in the dining room, taking two empty seats at the table by the fireplace.

"Rose, come join us," Lacey said to her daughter, who stood by the picture window gazing into the darkness.

"What's wrong, honey?" her dad asked.

"Oscar's missing," Lacey said.

"He's probably out chasing squirrels," Beau said.

"I saw him right before dinner," Chip offered.

"Where?" Rose asked.

"Barking at some guy near the stables," Chip said.

"What guy?" Rose said.

Chip shrugged. "The detective, I think?"

Jacob slowly put down his fork.

"Oscar wouldn't bark at T.J.," Rose said.

A pit formed in Jacob's gut. He stood and eyed the table across the room where the kids ate dinner. His gaze landed on an empty chair.

"Where's Miri?"

SEVEN

The room went eerily quiet.

The look on Jacob's face tore at Brianna's heart. Panic. Disbelief.

Utter devastation.

Brianna stood, both in solidarity because she wanted him to know he wasn't alone, but also because she needed to find the little girl and wipe that expression off his face.

"Chip, did you see Miri outside?" Brianna said.

Chip put down his fork. "I... I didn't notice, sorry."

The family shared looks of concern. Something sparked inside Brianna.

"Lacey and Bill, why don't you check her room and the playroom?" Brie said calmly. "Rose, contact the detective and determine if he was out here today. If he wasn't, explain what's happening. Beau, you check the barn," Brianna said.

"Hey, who made you—"

"Quiet," Jacob interrupted Beau.

Beau glared at Brie. "This is probably your fault."

"Beau, shush," his mother said, then turned to Brianna. "But if she's inside—"

"She might be hiding," Brie explained. "She was upset with her father today for not taking her owl hunting."

Lacey and Bill went to search the rooms.

Other guests offered to help.

"No, please remain here and finish your dinner," Brie said. "Once the house and barn are thoroughly checked, we may need your help searching the grounds."

She motioned for Jacob to follow her. She grabbed her jacket off the hook by the door and wrapped a scarf around her neck, unable to make eye contact with him. "Flashlights?"

He grabbed two off a table by the door. "I should have kept better track of her."

"Focus. Let's check the Little Wrangler's building. She probably went to make more bedding for her owl."

They opened the door to a cool burst of wind. She took a quick breath and walked toward the building where they held children's indoor activities."

"She's there. She's gotta be there," Jacob muttered.

"We'll find her," Brie said, because she wouldn't accept the alternative.

That Miri had been taken.

Because of Brie's presence at Boulder Creek Ranch.

She wouldn't allow that type of thinking to cloud her strategy. She'd always been the one to remain calm whether the news was bad or good. At the lab, Douglas was the one to dramatically celebrate their successes or sulk over their setbacks. And growing up, well, she wouldn't allow her aunt the power to know how Brie felt for fear Aunt Judith would use Brie's feelings as a weapon against her.

Brie might be presently challenged because of her head trauma, but the seriousness of Miri being taken snapped her into hyperfocus mode.

They approached the building, and she noticed a soft glow through the window. Jacob must have also seen it, because he quickly opened the door.

"Miri?"

The large, one-room building was empty. Jacob went to analyze materials at a workstation, while Brie scanned the room looking for some clue as to what happened.

"They're not supposed to leave the lights on," he said, picking up a drawing of an owl.

That's when Brie noticed seeds on the floor. She followed the trail, which led her to a metal cabinet. She opened the cabinet.

"Miri was here," she said.

"What? How do you know?" He crossed the room.

She pointed to the open bag of seeds.

"My guess? Miri took seeds to feed the owls."

"No, she wouldn't have... You think she went into the woods?"

"She was determined to hunt owls."

"Not at night."

"She may have discovered that many owl species are nocturnal and thought she'd have a better chance of finding one at night."

"In the dark?" he said, incredulous.

"She is five, not thirty-five. She doesn't think like you and me. She doesn't have the common sense of an adult."

"I know, but we have rules at the ranch, and not going out at night is one of them. I mean, she can't see anything at night."

Brie held up her flashlight.

"Do you really think that's what happened, or...?"

"Yes. Notify the family. We're going to fan out and find her."

Twenty minutes later, Lacey and Bill, Beau and Rose, and Jacob and Brie formed teams to explore the area surrounding the property. A few guest teams also formed to help with the search.

The little girl couldn't have gone far, Brie

thought. Miri was determined, but she was also smart, and Brie hoped that her intelligence would caution her not to wander too far away.

Then again, she was on a mission to find an owl.

As Brie and Jacob walked along the creek behind the ranch, she appreciated the nearly full moon that offered much-needed light for their hunt.

Jacob suddenly stopped.

"What?" Brie said.

He knelt down. When he stood, he held a pine-cone owl in his hand. "She never would have left this behind."

"She would if she thought she found something better."

Jacob turned and shouted, "Miri!"

"Miri!" Brie called out.

They continued along the trail. The trickle of rippling water against the rocks competed with Brie's ability to hear clearly, to listen for the sound of a child responding to her father's voice. If only Brie could turn off the sound of the water.

Focus on one thing at a time; block out everything else.

Her mentor Professor McMahon's words echoed back to her. She closed her eyes for a second.

Thought she heard something.

Faint and unclear, it could have been a sound from any number of animals.

She opened her eyes and took a few more steps, aiming her flashlight at the ground.

And spotted something. Brianna picked up a dog biscuit.

"She took Oscar with her." She showed Jacob the biscuit.

As if they'd read each other's minds, they both turned and called Oscar's name as they continued their search. Since dogs had better hearing, it was possible he'd hear their calls before Miri would.

"I'll text the group about Oscar." Jacob shot off a message to the family.

"Oscar!" Brie called. "Miri!"

Then she had a thought: the child would be looking up while walking along the trail and perhaps could have lost her footing and fallen into the creek. She quickly shelved that hypothesis, wanting to remain positive and work through all other possibilities before considering the more tragic ones.

Tragic?

"Miri!" Brie called. "Oscar!"

"The family's headed this way. They'll start at the other end of the trail and work their way towards us. She's been out here too long by herself," Jacob said.

As he picked up his pace, Brie lagged behind,

fearing if they went too fast in their desperation to find Miri, they might miss clues that could lead them to the little girl.

He glanced over his shoulder, as if not wanting to leave Brianna.

"Don't wait for me. Go on ahead," she encouraged him.

As Brie took measured steps, she imagined she was a little girl in search of a wide-eyed owl. She aimed the light up at a tree, then another, but saw nothing.

She sighed and closed her eyes again. Took a deep, cleansing breath.

Listened.

"Miri!" Jacob's voice echoed through the woods.

She quieted her mind and let her troubled thoughts drift past. Cocked her head slightly.

Hoot, hoot.

She opened her eyes and stepped off the trail. That sound would certainly have drawn Miri deeper into the woods.

"Oscar!" she called, hoping the dog would have the sense to respond.

A soft, throaty bark resonated through the forest. Brie pushed aside foliage and continued on her quest to find the little girl. What if the sound of the barking dog was misleading?

"Stay focused." As she struggled through the creeping juniper, she jerked the flashlight upward and spotted an owl glaring down at her.

This could be the reason why Miri had gone off the trail.

"Jacob!" she called.

Brie pushed through more brush, heading for the sound, the dog's barks getting louder, more excited.

And there, in the distance, she spotted Oscar.

Standing beside a curled-up ball of bright pink. Miri.

Brie choked back a gasp and practically sprinted to the child. As she approached, Brie dropped to her knees, breathing heavily.

"Jacob!" Brie cried, not knowing what else to do. The child needed her father.

Oscar stopped barking and looked at Brie, expectant. She offered him the biscuit she'd found. "Good boy, Oscar."

Brie touched the little girl's shoulder. "Miri?"

The girl sniffed.

"Honey, are you okay?" Brie said, the endearment rolling easily off her tongue.

"Yeah."

"Then why are you curled up in a ball?"

"I got lost. Oscar got lost, too."

"I know the way back. Let's go home."

The little girl straightened, threw her arms around Brie's neck and started crying.

"Hey, don't cry. You're safe now."

"Everyone's gonna be mad at me." Her voice

hitched. "Nanna and Gramps, Papa Beau and Auntie Rose. And Papa Jay is gonna be *really* mad."

"No, he's not," Jacob said from behind Brie.

Miri squeezed Brie tighter.

"Sweetie." Jacob knelt beside them. "I'm not angry. I'm upset. You know why?"

Miri sniffed.

"Because I love you," Jacob said. "I was so worried that you were hurt, and I couldn't get to you. Are you…hurt?"

"No," she said into Brianna's shoulder.

Jacob placed an open palm against her back. "You're the most precious thing in the world to me, Owl. You know that, right?"

She nodded.

"Ready to go home?" he said.

"Ye-ah."

She didn't release her hold on Brie.

"I've got her," Brie said softly to Jacob and stood with Miri in her arms.

"Your ankle—"

"It's better." And it was, but perhaps because the adrenaline rush masked everything else.

Brie might be in pain later, but she didn't care. The feeling of this little girl holding on to her warmed Brie's heart like nothing ever had before. A connection she'd ached for but had always been denied.

Yet she was offering it to another child.

Something shifted inside her, almost as if the skin was healing over an open wound.

Jacob walked beside them and caught Brianna's eye. "Say the word if she gets too heavy."

Oscar trotted a few feet ahead of them, leading the way home.

"It occurs to me that Oscar could have returned to the ranch, but he wouldn't leave Miri," Brie said.

"Good dog."

"He deserves a major reward."

"So do you."

"I didn't do anything."

She felt his hand on her shoulder. "You found my daughter. And then some."

Miri turned her head and released a sigh against Brianna's neck. A sigh of peace, contentment.

Brie's eyes misted with unshed tears.

Before they even reached the property, the rest of the family met them on the trail, peppering them with questions.

Jacob answered each and every one, relieved at how things had turned out and proud of Brianna's role in finding Miri. Each time someone offered to take Miri, his daughter shook her head and clung tighter to Brianna's neck. They'd developed a special connection. Jacob could tell Brianna felt it, too, and was hesitant to let go of his daughter.

When they reached the house, Jacob encouraged Brianna to pass Miri to him so he could get her ready for bed. He spent the next few hours loving on his daughter, getting her something to eat, helping her wash up, reexplaining why he was so upset, and then he took extra time tucking her in and reading to her.

It was early for her to go to sleep, but Miri was exhausted, in part from the residual effects of being terrified and alone in the woods.

After kissing her good night and giving her owl a kiss as well, Jacob shut her door and left the private wing of the house to join the others in the kitchen.

"We couldn't have found her without you." Lacey's voice drifted down the hallway.

"Her father would have found her, no doubt," Brianna responded.

"With a little help from Oscar," Rose said.

"He's quite a remarkable dog," Brianna said.

Jacob entered the kitchen and poured a cup of coffee. Rose was sitting at the kitchen island with Lacey, Brianna and Beau.

"Do you have anything you'd like to say to Brianna, *Papa Beau*?" Rose challenged her brother.

"Good job," Beau said.

"I was thinking more like an apology," Rose said.

"For what?"

Rose groaned.

"Beau," Lacey said, with warning in her voice.

Jacob leaned against the counter, enjoying the interaction.

"What?" Beau said. "I can't help it if I thought her problems put Miri at risk. I wasn't the only one at the table who thought that, right?" He aimed his question at Jacob. The three women turned and looked at him.

"Sorry, man, you're on your own," Jacob said.

"It never crossed your mind?"

"Nope. All I could think about was finding my little girl."

Awkward silence filled the kitchen.

"Then it looks like I'm the biggest jerk in the county." Beau walked his mug over to the sink and turned. "Sorry, Brianna."

"I understand. In your shoes, I probably would have assumed the same thing."

Beau put up his hand as if to say, *See, I'm not an idiot.*

"Go help your father with the campfire," his mother said, dismissing him.

"I'm always the bad guy," he muttered.

That got a chuckle out of Rose and her mom.

"How's our owl hunter?" Lacey asked Jacob.

"Exhausted, frustrated."

"Why, because she didn't find an owl?"

"She claims Oscar scared Mr. Owl off by barking."

"But I saw an owl in the trees above her," Brianna said.

"Anyway, she's also worried because I told her we'd discuss her punishment tomorrow," Jacob said. "I wanted to run it past you all first."

"You don't have to do that, Jacob," Lacey said. "You're her father. But if you'd like our feedback, we'd be glad to offer it, right, Rose?"

Rose's jaw dropped.

"What?" Lacey said.

Rose snapped her jaw shut. "Nothin'."

"What are you considering for her punishment?" Lacey said.

He noticed Brianna shift position and wince. He should escort her back to the cabin to rest her ankle. "Want me to take you back to your cabin?"

"In a few minutes, after I finish my tea," she said.

He sensed she liked the camaraderie of family.

"Well," he started, "I don't want to take Miri out of Little Wrangler's Club, because it's an enriching experience and keeps her busy. I thought, maybe, no dessert for five days, and no working in the barn until after church Sunday."

Lacey and Rose shared a look.

"What, too much?" Jacob said.

"Actually, that's quite fair," Lacey said.

"Not working in the barn is punishment?" Brie asked.

"It is when Miri's idea of working in the barn is to read to the horses."

"So...it's fun for her," Brie said.

"Yep."

"Oh, and it was in fact Detective Harper by the barn this afternoon. He was playing a hide-and-seek game with Oscar."

"He came out here to play with Oscar?" Lacey said.

"No, he stopped by to see me, but I was on the trail ride," Rose said.

"Why did he need to talk to you?" Lacey pressed.

Rose shrugged.

Assuming Rose didn't want an audience for the rest of this conversation, Jacob pushed away from the counter. "Done with your tea?" he said to Brianna.

"Yes." She picked up her mug.

"I'll take care of it," Lacey said. "Go on, get some rest."

Interesting. The house rule was to take care of your own dishes. Brianna had moved way up on Lacey's list.

"Thanks again for helping us find Miri," Lacey said to Brianna.

"My pleasure."

Jacob noticed a pleasant curl to Brianna's lips, and he couldn't help but smile. For some reason seeing this woman happy meant a lot to him. He caught himself. Was he feeling *too* connected to her emotional state? He'd better stop now before things got out of hand.

Before he developed feelings for a woman who'd be gone in a few days.

As they headed for her cabin, he spotted the glow of the campfire in the distance. The sound of Cowboy Joe's deep voice drifted across the property as adults and kids roasted marshmallows and made s'mores. It was a biweekly tradition, and one he and Miri rarely missed.

"Sounds like they're having fun," Brie said.

"We can go if you want, but I figured you were worn out," he said.

"I am, but thanks."

"Another time, then," he said, knowing there'd be no other time.

"I'm glad I was here, that I was able to help find Miri."

"She's really taken to you."

"She was scared. She would have reacted that way to any mother-type figure."

He stopped and touched her arm. "It's more than that. Nanna and Aunt Rose are great with her, but they're no substitute for a loving mother or even a mother like Cassie." He shook his head. "I shouldn't have said that. Sorry."

"What did you mean?"

"Apparently when Cassie moved back, she mostly let her family do the heavy lifting in regards to raising our daughter. Cassie wasn't around much, and even when she was...well, I get the impression she was disinterested in Miri."

"She was still Miri's mother, even if she wasn't perfect."

"Sounds like this is hitting close to home."

They continued toward the cabin. "After my sister died, Mother drank a lot, trying to numb the grief, I guess," Brie said. "No matter how hard I tried, I couldn't fix things, make her love me enough to move on." She looked at him. "But she was my mother, so I kept making excuses for her."

"You were giving her grace."

"Is that what it's called?"

"Yes. What about your dad?"

"He lost himself in work to avoid the pain. Then after Mother died, he drifted away, found a new wife and family. Basically abandoned me."

"Brianna, I am so sorry."

"I'm over it."

"I don't know if you ever really get over that kind of trauma."

She stopped suddenly, and he thought she might argue with him. Being a scientist, she probably had all kinds of intellectual answers to how someone heals from trauma. Instead, she pointed at her dark cabin. "I left the porch light on."

"Hang tight." Jacob went to the front porch. Peered inside the cabin with a small flashlight. "Everything looks good inside."

He turned.

And saw a man wrap one hand around Brie's mouth and the other around her waist.

"Let her go," Jacob demanded, launching off the porch.

He was grabbed from behind by a hefty guy who applied a headlock, restricting Jacob's movement.

Something pinched Jacob's neck, and he was shoved to the ground. As he tried to get up, the guy kicked him in the gut.

He could hear Brie's muffled protest against her attacker's palm. Jacob glanced at her.

"You'll keep quiet?" the guy said.

She nodded, and he removed his hand.

"Don't hurt him. Please, don't hurt him," she begged.

Jacob coughed and tried to stand again, but something slammed against his back, pinning him in place.

"Stay down," a deep voice ordered.

"I'll go with you," Brianna said. "Leave him here and I'll go without protest."

"No can do. He's coming with us."
And the world faded into a blur of nothingness.

EIGHT

"Why can't you leave him here? I said I'd go willingly," Brianna protested.

"We're not going to hurt you or your friend, but we need leverage, and we know you'll cooperate if we've got him."

That's when she realized the man restraining her was Eric from the mountains yesterday.

"A little help here?" Eric's partner said, trying to drag Jacob away.

"Let me get her into the car first." With a firm grip on Brie's arm, he led her behind the cabin to a black Suburban.

"Why are you doing this?" she said.

"My boss needs to talk to you."

"Who's your boss?"

"Save the questions." He opened the passenger door and motioned her inside the SUV. "Keep quiet. If you do anything stupid like honk the horn, your friend will suffer more than a hangover from the sedative."

He slammed the door.

She fisted her hands and released one of her muffled screams, the kind she'd perfected as a teen so no one would hear her, judge her and use her frustration against her.

"You're smart. Figure your way out of this," she said.

She didn't want to put Jacob in more danger, nor did she want to put the Rogers family or their guests at risk.

Knowledge was power, and she needed more of it.

She dug through the front seat's back pocket, looking for something to give her a clue about her captors, but she came up empty. If this was a rental, there wouldn't be much in the back seat. She leaned forward and spotted a notepad with words scribbled across the top: *Det. Harper— Dr. Wilkes at Boulder Creek Ranch.*

Wait, what? Detective Harper was involved in this?

The door opened, and the men awkwardly shoved Jacob into the back, his head flopping against the headrest.

Eric looked across Jacob at Brie and said, "To be clear, we're going to leave the property without incident. If you do anything to prevent that, well—" he gently slapped Jacob's cheek "—your cowboy will suffer the consequences."

* * *

Help! Somebody help me!

Jacob was walking down a long, dark hallway, passing what looked like classrooms in a school. A light flickered in the distance, then went dark.

Had to get to her. Had to save...who? Kara Roberts?

He sprinted to the end of the hallway and flung open the red door.

Froze at the sight of Kara, floating on a pile of hay. Dead.

Help me! Please! Someone cried from another room.

Jacob spun around and went in search of the voice, his boots slipping on what felt like black ice.

Here! I'm in here!

A door opened at the end of the hall. Cassie stood there, her arms stiff by her side.

Then she shifted Miri in front of her. "I'm taking her with me."

"No, Cassie!" Jacob said.

"Daddy! I want Daddy," Miri cried.

The door slammed shut.

He scrambled to get to his child and skidded, crashing into the door. He pounded on it with closed fists. "Miri!"

A woman laughed behind him. He jerked around.

Cassie stood there, holding on to a sobbing Miri. "You can't save her. No one can."

"No! No, Miri!" He lunged for his daughter, but she evaporated like the morning mist. "Where are you, Miri?" he cried out. "Miri!"

"Jacob! Wake up!"

A sting startled him awake. He struggled to breathe against the pain of a headache worse than any he'd ever had. Opening his eyes, he saw Brianna kneeling next to him.

"Sorry about the slap," she said. "You were having an intense nightmare."

He nodded, relieved that's all it was, that he hadn't lost his daughter…again.

Then he looked beyond Brianna, and struggled to recognize his surroundings.

"They said you might need this." She handed him acetaminophen and reached for a water bottle on a nearby desk.

"Who are they?"

"Still not sure. We're in an airplane hangar waiting for their boss to arrive."

He struggled to open the bottle of pain reliever.

"Here." She took it from him, popped the top off and handed him two pills.

"What did they give me?" He pressed the heel of his palm against his temple.

"I don't know, but you've been out for hours."

He snapped his gaze to her. "You're okay? They didn't hurt you?"

"No, but they threatened to hurt you if I refused to cooperate."

"Me? Why?"

"You're the closest thing I have to a friend in town, and I probably exposed my feelings when I begged them to leave you behind."

"Thanks for trying."

"I couldn't bear the thought of taking Miri's father away from her."

He nodded. "Right."

So, she hadn't *begged* them to leave Jacob behind because she cared about him. This was about Miri. Good to know.

"Did I say something wrong?" she said.

He ignored the question. "You said we're in an airplane hangar?"

"Yes, in the upstairs office."

"Are they taking us somewhere?"

"I don't think so. They locked us in here until their boss arrives."

He rubbed his temples.

"I am very sorry."

"Me, too."

"What are you sorry about?"

"For not protecting you."

"There were two of them, and they caught us off guard. Who could have possibly known they'd come for me at a ranch full of people?"

"I guess protecting you there wasn't such a great idea after all."

"Because they got my location from the detective."

Squinting against his throbbing headache, Jacob looked at her. She seemed calmer, more clearheaded than most people would be in her situation. She was definitely more grounded than when he'd pulled her out of the river.

"Wait, what did you say?" he said.

"They had help from the detective."

"Detective Harper?"

She nodded. "I saw his name written on a notepad in their truck, next to the words *Boulder Creek Ranch*."

"I find that hard to believe."

"It's the only way they could have found me. I wasn't using my real name."

"We've gotta get out of here."

He stood and wavered, leaning into the desk. "I assume they took our cell phones?"

"And removed the phone from this office. There were employees working in the hangar, but when I banged on the window, they ignored me."

"Hang on, you were the one calling for help?" The cries had seeped into his dream.

"Yes, a waste of energy."

"Then we'll figure out another way." He took a few steps toward the door and struggled to stay upright.

"Jacob, sit down." She took his arm and led him to an office chair.

He pinched his eyes shut. "So, is it a double lock? A lock on both sides of the door?"

"Yes."

"Good. Check the desk drawers for something sharp, a letter opener or paper clip."

Massaging his temples, he admitted he wasn't going anywhere soon. He'd have to convince Brianna to leave him behind and get help.

"I found paper clips."

"Good. Uncurl two and hand them to me."

He opened his eyes and rolled his chair over to the lock. He reconfigured one paper clip to resemble a lock-picking tool that would ideally hold the tumblers in place and stuck the other one into the lock to bend the tip just so.

"You're picking the lock?" she said.

"Gonna try."

"And you know how to do this, why?"

"I was a precocious teenager."

"That must be where your daughter gets it."

He smiled. "Let's hope she gets only the good stuff, not this."

"If this works, that would be pretty good."

Focused on his task, he moved the second paper clip right, then left. "This might take a while."

He kept at it, desperate to free them, or at least

free Brianna. He wasn't sure how far he'd get in this state and didn't want to slow her down.

She must have thought he needed to concentrate, because she was completely silent for the twenty minutes it took him to pick the lock.

"You really did it," Brianna said with awe in her voice when the knob turned easily.

"Hidden talents." He swung open the door and peered left, then right. "Now go. Go get help."

Instead, she took a step back into the office. "You're coming with me."

"I can barely walk."

"I'll help you."

"My head feels like it's stuffed with oatmeal. I'm not stable. Now go."

"I'm not leaving you."

"Don't be foolish." He mentally scolded himself and tried again, using better, kinder words. "You can figure out a way to contact police, tell them where we are."

"I have no idea where we are," she said. "And by the time I figure it out and they arrive, you could be—"

"They haven't killed anyone yet. I doubt they're going to start now."

She paled, his harsh words sabotaging his case to get her to leave. But then, he was running on low cognitive function thanks to whatever drug they'd given him.

"Please, just go get help," he tried again.

She studied him with regret in her eyes, and for a second he thought he'd convinced her to leave.

Instead, she shut the door. "They have repeatedly said they don't want to hurt me."

"That's what they all say," he muttered, collapsing in the office chair.

"Why go to all the trouble of kidnapping both of us and holding us hostage? You're right—if they wanted to kill us, they would have done so. They want something from me, and I won't give it to them unless they let you go."

"Brianna—"

"You're here because of me. You're—" her voice caught "—hurt because of me."

"No, sweetheart." The endearment slipped out as he reached forward and took her hands in his. "Look at me."

She pursed her lips and shook her head.

"Brianna?"

Slowly, those caramel-colored eyes met his. He gave her hands a gentle squeeze.

"None of this is your fault," he said. "You didn't do anything wrong—you didn't hurt anyone. You're devoted to your work that will help millions of people, and for whatever reason, that has put a bull's-eye on your back."

Her gaze drifted downward.

"Brianna?"

"It feels like my fault," she said softly. "You're

a nice man with a little girl and a family that loves you, and I'm ruining that, too." She slipped her hand from his and went to the other side of the office, gazing into the hangar below.

"I don't know what the adults in your life told you growing up, but know this—adults are not necessarily right, and they don't always speak the truth. Perhaps it's the truth from their perspective, but it's not the truth from the child's. Understand?"

She nodded.

Suddenly the door opened. "Mr. Jenson will see you now," Eric said.

Jacob stood.

"Just Dr. Wilkes."

"Oh no, he goes where I go," Brianna said.

"It's fine, I probably couldn't make it anyway." Jacob plopped back in the chair.

Eric motioned to Brianna. She crossed her arms over her chest. "Enough of the bullying tactics, Eric. You said you're not going to hurt me, but this hurts me, seeing Jacob like this. Do know he has a little girl?"

"This has nothing to—"

"It's time we all start acting like adults and respect each other's positions. I will gladly come talk to your boss if Jacob accompanies me. It was, after all, your idea to bring him here." She went to Jacob's side and helped him stand. "Ready?"

"This involves your work, Dr. Wilkes. My boss may not want strangers being privy to your conversation."

"Jacob is not a stranger, he's my friend and a social worker. He knows how to keep a confidence."

As Brianna and Jacob were guided down the stairs and through the hangar, Brie questioned her decision to bring Jacob with her. Would it have been better to leave him behind so he could escape on his own? Was she being selfish by dragging him along to the meeting?

No, her intention had been good. She wanted to keep him close to make sure he wasn't being hurt. Or was it something else? The stability and maybe even the confidence boost she felt whenever he was close? These feelings were foreign to Brianna, so she chalked it up to the head trauma, an excuse that was starting to feel hollow.

They exited the building, and she spotted a plane a few hundred feet away. Now she was really worried. If this mysterious Jenson character decided to take Brianna with him to parts unknown, what would happen to Jacob? How could she protect him from these men if they were separated?

She remembered when Miri had buried her head against Brie's neck, the warmth, the trust she felt from the child.

Had it been misplaced? Brie detested feeling like a failure, like she'd let people down. She obviously hadn't done enough to save her mother nor had Brie been enough to keep her father around.

And now it seemed that she wasn't clever enough to protect Jacob.

"Whatever you're thinking, stop," Jacob said.

She eyed him. "How did you…?"

"Social worker, remember?" He smiled.

Somehow that reserved smile gave her strength to think more clearly.

She focused on gaining their freedom. They approached the steps to the plane, and she said to Eric, "I can't fly due to my concussion."

"There's no flight plan. Not yet, anyway."

She helped Jacob up the steps. By the time they boarded the plane, his breathing was labored and his pulse had increased. Gripping his arm, she helped him to a plush chair on the plane and sat next to him.

"Mr. Jenson will be here soon," Eric said.

"Super," Brie muttered.

A young man wearing navy blue pants and a white shirt and tie came to greet them. He offered a pleasant smile. "Would you like anything to drink?"

"Are you kidding?" Brianna said.

The young man's smile faded.

"Sure, I'll have a coffee and she'll have…?" Jacob looked at Brianna.

"Ginger ale," she said.

With a nod, the man went to the galley.

She peered out the window into the darkness. If there *was* a God, she hoped he wouldn't allow these men to hurt Jacob.

Jacob's God, can you hear me? Please protect him from my own stupidity.

Jacob's warm hand touched hers. "Have a little faith."

She almost laughed. If he only knew what she'd been thinking.

"Dr. Wilkes," a tall man greeted. Sharply dressed, he was in his midforties. "It's good to meet you finally. I'm Nathaniel Jenson." He offered his hand.

She declined to shake it.

"I apologize about our strategy to get you here, and any discomfort," he said to Jacob.

"You're sorry? Your men tried to kidnap me yesterday and succeeded today," Brie countered.

Mr. Jenson sat across from them. "For your own good."

"That's ridiculous."

Jacob shot her a look.

"Mr. Jenson, I'm tired and frustrated," Brie started. "I don't know you and I certainly don't need your protection when you are, in fact, the one who's been trying to kidnap me."

Jenson shot Jacob a raised eyebrow. "Gutsy."

"Brain injury?" Jacob shrugged.

"Anger," she corrected them both. Glaring at Jenson, she said, "What do you want?"

"For one, I've been trying to get a private meeting with you for months."

"Why?"

The flight attendant returned with their drinks and handed Mr. Jenson an envelope.

"Thank you, Logan." Mr. Jenson passed the envelope to Brianna. "Go ahead, take a look."

She pulled out a photograph of a blond-haired little girl with freckles, lying in a hospital bed with an IV inserted into her arm. "Who is this?"

"Cynthia, my daughter. She suffers from a rare autoimmune disease, one that will follow her into adulthood. One that could, potentially, kill her."

The slight crack in his voice softened Brie's irritation.

"I'm sorry," she said.

He leaned forward. "She suffers terrible side effects from the drugs they're using to treat her. I know you're close to developing alternatives to the medications she's being prescribed."

Brie's heart ached for him. In truth she wished she could focus on children as subjects, but her funding had been to study the adult population.

"Mr. Jenson, we haven't focused on children in our research. It would be inappropriate to assume our conclusions would hold true for children without having completed proper studies and trials."

Mr. Jenson sighed. "Is that why you refused my meetings over the past few months?"

"I... I'm sorry if I declined meeting with you, but my response would have been the same."

"*If* you declined? You don't remember?"

She glanced at Jacob, who offered a supportive nod. He wasn't the type of man to lie and had just spoken about adults not telling the truth.

"I am struggling with some memory issues," she admitted. "I'm sorry if I evaded your requests for a meeting, but it's inappropriate for me to speak with random strangers about my research."

"I'm not a random stranger. I'm the biggest anonymous donor of the study."

"Oh. Well, thank you for that." She took a deep breath. "But it still doesn't give you the right to kidnap me."

"Again, my apologies. I sent my men to protect you because you're in danger."

"From threatening emails?"

"It's bigger than that."

"Meaning?"

"Do you remember the near hit-and-run last month when you were crossing the street, or the doorman being assaulted at your apartment building?"

Anxiety fluttered in her belly. How could she

not remember these events? Or had she subconsciously blocked them out after suffering the head injury?

"Brianna?" Jacob said, searching her eyes.

She shook her head.

"Wait a minute, that man named Stan, does he also work for you?" she asked Mr. Jenson.

"I don't employ anyone named Stan."

"Why am I in danger for wanting to help people heal?"

"It could put some very powerful people out of business." Mr. Jenson motioned for Logan to bring him a beverage. "Drug companies, investors who make billions off pharmaceutical sales. Your research could greatly impact their bottom line. I've also heard someone is sponsoring a competing study, one that plans to monetize its findings."

"Monetize methods to naturally trigger self-healing? How would you even do that?"

"Claim to have better, more effective techniques than your study, hire and send employees to train others. People would pay to become coaches, pay for training materials. They'd host retreats, build websites offering sales of their own line of products and services, and so on."

"My goal is to make our protocol available to anyone who needs it to heal, cost-free."

"I understand. But not everyone agrees with

your strategy. Then there are rumors that you've been intentionally holding back for publicity purposes."

"Publicity?"

"To time your release with the International Science Awards Symposium, reveal your great achievement in a grand way, get published and be respected by the science community."

"I have no interest in that kind of recognition. All I care about is making people better."

"Even children?"

"Of course, eventually I'd like to focus my study on kids as well."

"Is it true that you've secretly completed your findings and are ready to present?"

"I can't say for sure."

"I'm your primary donor."

"Then I hate to admit this to you, but I'm not clear about our conclusions because of my head injury."

"Oh, I see."

If Mr. Jenson shared that nugget of information with the head of the Viceroy Foundation, she'd be out of a job, her work scrapped and her reputation ruined.

"Once we've concluded our research, I am going to propose a new study for children," Brie said.

"You're just saying that to appease me."

"No, I'm telling you something I've never admitted to my colleagues. Studying children's autoimmune disease and how to help them has always been my ultimate goal." She sighed. "My sister suffered from juvenile Addison's disease, among other things. She died when I was ten."

She felt Jacob's comforting hand on her shoulder.

"Since there are more adults with autoimmune diseases than children and I had to fund my research, I started with adults."

"And your memory, is it…?"

"Things are slowly coming back to me. Rest and relaxation would help, but that hasn't happened since my fall."

"No, and that's partly my fault," Mr. Jenson said. "Again, my intentions were honorable, to protect you and your research."

"I felt protected and safe at the ranch until your men found me. Detective Harper works for you as well? He told you where I was staying?"

"No, my men discovered he was investigating the break-in at your motel and tracked his vehicle, assuming he'd meet with you in person at some point. When he went to the ranch, they followed."

"I see. So, anyone could do the same thing?"

"Doubtful. My security team has very sophisticated tracking equipment. However, it would reduce the possibility of anyone else discovering your location if the detective refrained from interviewing you at the ranch. Actually, it would be wiser to return with me to Chicago."

"Would it?" she countered. "It doesn't sound like I'm all that safe back home. At least here I can be someone else for a few days, which will give me time to investigate."

"Investigate?"

"Who's behind these threats. Back at the lab I wouldn't have the time. I'll be safe at the ranch and can covertly investigate who's after me and why."

"Well, when you are ready to return, please contact me and I'll send my private jet. In the meantime, shall I leave my men in town to protect you?"

"No, thank you. They'll only draw more attention to my presence. Now, I'd like to go home— I mean, to the ranch." She glanced at Jacob. His chin was lowered and his eyes closed. He'd fallen asleep.

"He'll be fine in the morning," Mr. Jenson said.

"Hoot-hoot. Hoot-hoot."

Jacob slowly opened his eyes. He was in his own bed at the ranch.

"Hoot-hoot," Miri whispered by his ear, her breath warming his cheek.

He grabbed her and held her close. He was home, safe, with his daughter in his arms. Had any of it happened? Being drugged, kidnapped and questioned?

"Papa Jay, you're squeezing the stuffing out of me," she said against his shoulder.

"Sorry, Owl. I missed you."

She leaned back. "I'm supposed to ignore you all day today."

"Yeah, why's that?"

"You didn't come save me from the leopard with purple spots."

"The what?"

"My nightmare. I ran into your room, and you weren't there. Papa Beau had to save me."

Someone cleared her throat from the doorway. Jacob looked up at Rose. "Oh, hey."

"Okay, little owl—"

"I'm a big owl!" Miri corrected her aunt.

"Sorry, big owl, go get some breakfast while I talk to Papa Jay."

Miri planted a wet kiss on Jacob's cheek and rushed out of the room.

Jacob sat up and realized he was still in his clothes from last night. He released a deep sigh.

"Someone's in trou-ble," she said in a sing-song voice. "Spend the night at the Alpine Cabin, did you?"

"No, and don't start rumors."

"Is he awake?" Beau bellowed from the hall-way.

"Oh, boy, here it comes," she said to Jacob. "Good luck."

Beau pushed past her into the bedroom and hovered over Jacob. "What happened to you last night? Too busy flirting with the scientist to comfort your little girl?"

"He said that's not what he was doing," Rose defended.

"I don't care what he was doing, I'm about this close to—"

"We were kidnapped," Jacob said.

That shut Beau up, but only for a second. "Now what trouble did she bring to the ranch?"

"She didn't bring it. Detective Harper did, un-intentionally."

"What do you mean?" Rose said.

"When he came out here yesterday. Some guys had planted a tracking device on his car so they'd know where to find Brianna."

"Oh, no." Rose framed her cheeks with her hands.

"It's not his fault," Jacob said.

"No, it's your fault, Detroit," Beau said. "For bringing that woman here and exposing us to who knows what."

"We have a pretty good idea what it's all about now," Jacob said.

"Wait, if you were kidnapped, how did you end up back here?" Rose said.

"They brought us back after they grilled Brianna for information about her research. It's a long story. I'll let her tell it if she wants to."

"She'd better want to since we're offering her a safe place to hide out and all she's done is cause trouble."

Jacob glared at Beau. "She found Miri last night."

Beau clenched his jaw. "We would have found her eventually."

"I need to clean up." Jacob stood. He didn't have the time or patience to spar with Beau.

"If anything happens to that little girl—"

"Enough!" Jacob shouted at Miri's uncle. "No one's after Miri. They're after Brianna because she's devoted her life to helping people. She's not the bad guy here, Beau. Besides, if anything happened to Miri, I'd cease to exist. Got it?"

Beau didn't move. His left eye twitched.

"Look, I wouldn't let Brianna stay if I thought it was putting Miri, or any of you, in serious danger. Now however much I enjoy my new siblings, please, could both of you leave?"

Beau snorted and stormed away.

"I'm sorry that they found Brianna because T.J. came out here yesterday," Rose said.

"Only doing his job."

"No, he came out here to see me."

"Well, we're safe now."

"But the kidnappers…?"

"They work for a guy who turned out to be more friend than foe—at least, it seems that way."

"Good. Okay. I'll go check on Miri."

"Thanks. I really appreciate all you do for her."

"My pleasure."

"How's Brianna today?"

"I haven't seen her yet."

With a nod, Jacob went about getting ready for the day. The cool shower helped him clear the crud from his brain. Man, whatever drug they'd given him, it felt like he'd be fighting the effects for days. Not good when you had a physical job, a child to care for and a friend to protect.

Friends—that's all he and Brianna could ever be.

Ambling into the kitchen, he grabbed a cran-berry-orange scone, poured coffee into a dispos-able cup and was about to head out when Lacey intercepted him.

"You weren't here for your daughter last night."

The words, again pointing out his failure, felt like a gut punch.

Jacob calmly explained what happened, how they'd been kidnapped in order to meet with some rich guy about Brianna's work.

"Oh, Jacob," she said with what he interpreted as censure in her voice.

"I understand if you no longer want her to stay," he said, although he wasn't sure how he'd break it to her.

Or how he'd say goodbye. He chided himself for having these kinds of feelings for a stranger who would leave as soon as she was able. Perhaps it was best to start building some distance between them.

"Is she still in danger?" Lacey said.

"Yes, but not from the men who kidnapped us last night. Others—we don't know who, exactly. All because she wants to help people." He shook his head. "Anyway, I understand if you want her to leave."

"And go where?"

He shrugged.

"Let's not make any rash decisions just yet."

"I've gotta get to the barn."

"All right," she said with a concerned frown. "Jacob?"

"Yes, ma'am."

"I do respect you for wanting to help Brianna."

"Thanks. Not everyone in the family shares your opinion."

"We'll talk later."

With a nod he left the house. As he headed toward the barn, he cast a quick glance toward the Alpine Cabin. Brianna's curtains were closed, and the morning basket with pastries and the coffee thermos sat by her door, untouched. Good, she deserved to sleep in, to sleep all day if she wanted.

He hoped she'd remain at the ranch, where she'd be anonymous and safe, that the family would support his need to save a stranger.

A stranger who was doing noble work to help others. She might not believe in God, but Brianna lived her life to help people. Jacob admired that, especially since her life's work had put her own life in jeopardy.

Jacob didn't know many people like Brianna.

Since they'd already brought the horses down from the pasture, Jacob helped get the trail rides organized. When Beau assigned a junior wrangler to follow the back of his group instead of Jacob, he got the message that he'd been relegated to grunt work for the day. No problem. Jacob didn't want to be in Beau's company, with his judgmental stare and acerbic tone.

By lunchtime Jacob felt like he'd worked a full day.

He headed for the main house to help with lunch and spotted the food basket and thermos on Brianna's porch. Deciding to check in, he approached the cabin and realized the basket hadn't been touched, the plaid cloth still perfectly folded in classic Lacey Rogers style.

He tapped softly on the cabin door. "Brianna? It's Jacob."

No response.

"Hey sleepy lady, time to get up and have something to eat."

Nothing.

"Brianna?" He knocked harder, then tried peering through the lace curtains, but he couldn't see anything.

"Papa Jay?" Miri said.

He turned around. "Hey, baby girl, whatcha doin' here?"

"Owl has something for you." She thrust her hand out. He took a white note from her little fingers. "She's gone, too."

He opened it.

I'm sorry about last night. I will not put you or your family in danger again. Don't try to find me. —Brianna

NINE

It was the right thing to do.

As Brianna logged on to the computer at the university, she fought the shame of leaving without saying goodbye in person. But she knew Jacob would try to convince her to stay, and he might have succeeded.

She'd covertly hitched a ride off the property with the dairy truck, and Andrea from the university where Brianna had spoken was kind enough to pick her up outside town.

Brie didn't want to conduct her investigation from the ranch's computer. She didn't know how tech savvy her enemies were and had to assume they could find her by tracing the IP address.

Her enemies. Who were they?

The only person who knew Brianna's whereabouts was Andrea. Brie didn't notify the detective in case his phone was being tapped. Now she was being paranoid.

No, she couldn't be too careful.

Which was why she tucked her hair in a base-ball cap and did everything in her power to look like a typical college student. Andrea reserved Brianna a private room with a personal computer for the day and offered to drive Brie to the ranch or drop her at a local inn when she was done.

But Brie didn't want to risk putting Jacob in danger again. The image of his unconscious body in the truck last night haunted her dreams and riddled her with guilt. She decided she'd stay in town in order to protect him.

This was getting complicated and confusing. She cared about Jacob, more than she should. Worse, she was starting to depend on him.

Perhaps she should see the doctor and get his approval to fly. Or maybe she could rent a car and drive back to Chicago. Yet, living in the city, she'd had little use for a car and seldom drove. The thought of a nearly twenty-four-hour drive from Montana to Chicago didn't seem wise.

"Stay focused," she said, eyeing the computer screen.

Andrea had given Brie a notebook and pen so she could jot down anything that seemed odd, along with the names of people who had threat-ened her via email.

Her plan had been to make the healing pro-tocol for autoimmune disease widely available, at which point there'd be no reason for anyone to harm her trying to get it before it became public. She wondered if the personal threats of the last few days indicated her lab was close to completing the project, thereby threatening drug companies.

After going through emails and making a few notes, she focused on her lab's encrypted research data. Using her private master passcode, she accessed the files to refamiliarize herself with the project.

She quickly became absorbed in the theoretical framework, study results and initial conclusions. "'Statistically significant metrics indicate a 50 percent decrease in antibodies,'" she read aloud. "That's remarkable." Although she didn't remember writing it.

Later in the afternoon, she uncovered an email that stopped her cold. It was from a drug company, offering to buy her research for a generous sum.

Brie's response email stated she would be happy to discuss.

"A drug company would bury it." She leaned back in her chair, feeling like she'd stepped into someone else's life, like she didn't recognize herself.

At all. A pit formed in her stomach. "Why can't I remember?"

Maybe she didn't want to because on some level she knew her actions were...deplorable?

Someone tapped on the door, and Andrea

popped her head into the room. "Not sure if you're done, but I'm leaving in ten minutes if you need a ride."

"That would be great."

"Meet me at the car."

"Thanks."

She closed her computer files and signed off. If only she had someone to talk to, someone who knew her and could counsel Brie about what to do next.

Someone like Jacob.

"You've only known him two days." She had a pretty good idea what he'd counsel in this situation: *pray.*

For the first time in her life she considered it, ached to surrender her internal conflict to a higher power.

"God, please help me."

Then she felt guilty about the request, since up to now she'd shut God out of her life. Jacob said God loved all His children. Brie could only hope that was true.

She stood and wavered, realizing she'd only eaten a protein bar for breakfast and had skipped lunch.

She'd better find a vending machine on her way out and grab something to raise her blood sugar. As she crossed the media center, she noticed the college students grouped together, some studying, some softly chuckling. Life had been so straightforward for Brie in school. Get good grades, earn her bachelor's degree, master's degree and then her doctorate.

Was Brie the same driven woman of integrity she'd been back then, or had something changed? Maybe the frustration of not making a difference fast enough had driven her away from her goal? No, Brianna prided herself on being patient, especially regarding her work. Then why would she sabotage it by selling her findings to a drug company?

She stopped at the vending machine, inserted the university card Andrea had given her to use on campus and bought a nut bar, the best choice of snack items from the candies and chips. Her cap pulled snugly over her forehead, she headed downstairs to the employee parking lot.

Although she ached to go back to the ranch, she resisted the temptation, and not only because of the potential danger shadowing her.

She felt ashamed. Ashamed of what she'd learned about herself today. Unlike Jacob, it appeared Brianna was not a good person, not if she was going to accept money to bury her research.

"There's got to be something missing."

Pushing the door open to the back lot, she headed in the direction of Andrea's car when the sound of a man's voice caught her attention. She glimpsed left and spotted a young man, perhaps in his teens, shouting at a woman as she walked away from him.

He violently yanked on her arm and spun her around. "Listen to me!"

Brianna's first reaction was to drop out of sight and wait for the danger to pass.

To do nothing.

"No," she ground out.

She ran back into the building and approached an open office door.

"Call security," she said to a woman behind the desk.

"What…?"

"Employee parking lot. I think a woman's being assaulted."

Brianna headed back outside to help, although she had no idea how. The young man was still shouting at the woman, who was now cowering beside a car.

"C'mon," Brie whispered, scanning the parking lot for security.

No security, no one to help.

Just as Jacob had been in the mountains at the right time to save Brianna, perhaps Brie was here to help a stranger.

What would Jacob do? He would intervene somehow, deescalate the situation.

She headed toward them and took out her phone, pretending to be absorbed in a text. She needed to be nonthreatening, buy time until help arrived.

She needed to disengage the young man from his anger and get him focused on something else.

Brie approached the couple, her eyes glued to her screen. "Do either of you know where the chemistry lab is?"

"Get back!" the young man shouted.

Startled, she looked up.

And saw he was clutching a gun.

This wasn't happening again.

Brianna was gone, too.

At first, Jacob couldn't believe she'd chosen to leave of her own free will. He feared someone had kidnapped her.

But the handwriting looked deliberate, not forced.

Jacob had been stewing over Brianna's decision when Lacey confronted him in the kitchen about his mood. Jacob told her Brianna had left a cordial note and abandoned him and Miri. Lacey challenged Jacob about his reaction, and he confessed Brianna's behavior had triggered the pain of losing Cassie.

"You...you really loved my daughter," Lacey said.

"Yes, ma'am. I kick myself every day for not seeing how my words and actions drove her away."

Lacey placed a comforting hand on his shoulder. "It takes two to build a relationship, Jacob."

He nodded.

"You're worried about Brianna?"

"Yes, ma'am. I feel like God wouldn't have let me save her from the river and these violent men only to have her kidnapped in town because she wanted to protect all of us."

"Then go find her. Remind her we can take care of ourselves. Invite her back, but don't force the issue. She seems like the type of woman who will push back if she doesn't feel respected."

"Agreed. What about my afternoon chores?"

"Go on, I'll get them covered."

Twenty minutes later he was headed to town. Having Lacey's support made all the difference and gave him the impetus to go after Brianna.

Jacob notified Detective Harper about Brianna's situation, and Harper said he'd help track her down.

This time the abandonment felt different, maybe even worse, because Brianna had abandoned Miri as well. Earlier this morning, his little girl had looked at him with such sad green eyes and said Dr. Wilkes had left, just like Mama.

Miri had bonded with Brianna in a way that caused heartbreak and triggered anger in Jacob. It was one thing to abandon Jacob, but Brianna had hurt his little girl.

Yet that wasn't the primary reason he wanted

to find her. Jacob sensed she was still a little off due to the head injury, and he feared she'd walk into trouble or make a bad decision…

Like Cassie had.

"No." He squeezed the steering wheel.

This had nothing to do with Cassie. Yet hadn't he admitted as much to Lacey? He could tell himself over and over that the trauma of losing Cassie, twice—when she left him and then when he learned she'd died—wasn't behind his determination to find Brianna and give her a piece of his mind about leaving Miri. The more he pushed that thought down, the more powerful it became.

This anger was so unlike Jacob.

Or was it?

He sighed and admitted that although the faithful Jacob wouldn't be consumed by darkness, his previous self had most definitely plummeted down that slippery slope. After Kara Roberts had died in his arms and Cassie had abandoned him, he couldn't hide from the rage or depression that followed.

And then, only God could save him from the depths of despair.

"Help me, Lord," he said. "Help me release this anger and replace it with something more…"

More what?

"Help me release this anger, and fill my heart with compassion."

He knew better than most that trauma had a

way of settling in your body no matter how many times you called it out. Still, he had to try.

Fill my heart with compassion.

He silently repeated his request as he drove to the university. He'd already learned that someone had seen a woman hitch a ride on the dairy truck this morning. That had to have been Brianna. And Brianna had mentioned being invited to speak at the university by someone named Andrea Carp. He'd tracked down her contact information, including her office location. Thinking she was the only other person Brianna knew in town, Andrea was his best shot of finding Brianna.

He pressed the call button for Andrea's office, but it went into voice mail. He'd already left two messages.

His phone rang with an incoming call, a blocked number.

"This is Jacob," he said.

"It's Harper. I'm on my way to the university."

"You figured it out, too?"

"What?"

"I'm guessing Brianna reached out to her contact at the university, Andrea Carp," Jacob said. "I'm almost there."

"I'm five minutes away. Wait for me outside the D building."

"I'll try."

"That's an order."

"I'm no longer a sworn officer, remember?"

"Smart guy."

"Not always." He ended the call and turned onto the main university drive. He'd taught a continuing ed class last semester on communication skills, so he knew the staff parking lot was in back. He'd found Andrea's photo online and noticed she taught a class in the afternoon. He'd wait for her to leave the building to approach her about Brianna. A part of him expected Brianna to be with her.

As he pulled around to the back, he saw a few students running frantically through the lot. He slowed down and lowered his window.

"What's going on?" he asked one of the kids.

"A guy with a gun!" she said, running past him.

Jacob slowly headed toward the commotion and called Detective Harper. "We've got a situation."

"I know. Gunman on campus. I'm pulling in now."

"I'm at the south end of the staff parking lot."

"I'll come from the north and send backup deputies to you," Harper said.

"Remind them I'm one of the good guys?"

"Ten-four."

Jacob ended the call, parked and carefully made his way through the lot, using cars as cover. With his training he might be able to defuse the situation before anyone got hurt. He peered around a compact car at the gunman.

And saw Brianna lying motionless on the ground.

Jacob dropped out of sight. "No, no, no," he whispered.

"Why won't you help me?" the gunman said, his voice cracking. He sounded like a desperate teen in pain.

Jacob took a deep breath and stood. Raising his hands in a gesture of surrender, he approached the gunman, who was definitely a teenager. An older woman, in her fifties, held her briefcase against her chest.

"Excuse me?" Jacob called out.

The teenager aimed the gun in Jacob's direction.

Have faith, Jacob coached himself.

"How can I help?" Jacob said.

"What?" the kid said.

"I'd like to help you."

"Why?"

"That's what I do."

"You're a cop?"

"No, not a cop."

"She's the only one who can help me." He nodded at the older woman, and she whimpered.

"I'd like to work this out for you, but first I need to check on that lady." He nodded at Brianna.

"I didn't shoot her," the kid said in a defensive tone.

"I believe you. So, what happened?"

"She...she just fainted."

"Would you mind if I gave her a look?"

The kid nodded. He seemed nervous, almost as if things were speeding out of control and he didn't know how to hit the brakes.

Jacob knelt beside Brianna and checked her for injuries, specifically a bullet wound.

"I told you I didn't shoot her."

"I'm looking for other injuries," Jacob said. "She's a friend of mine and suffered a head injury the other day." He glanced at the kid. "You don't want to mess with head injuries. I'll need to get her to the hospital. Emergency won't come back here if you're holding that." He nodded at the gun. "So, what's going on with you? Why the gun?"

"She won't return my calls!" he shouted at the older woman.

"What do you need to talk about?" Jacob said.

"She has to approve my application for the engineering program."

"But she can't talk to you if you're pointing a gun at her. How about you give it to me?"

"You're trying to trick me."

"No tricks. I'm trying to help you. Honest."

"You just want my gun."

"Buddy, I hate guns. More than you could possibly know. I'd also hate to see you ruin your life because of a misunderstanding. Give me the gun so I can get Brianna to the hospital, and you can set up a meeting with…?" He looked at the woman.

"Julie Denali," she said.

"And what's your name?" Jacob asked the teen.

"Pete. I… I need to get into the engineering school so I can get out of that house."

"What's the holdup? Have you got the grades?"

"Yeah."

"Then…?"

His eyes teared up. "My dad gambled away my college fund at the casino."

Jacob sighed. "I'm sorry, Pete. That's terrible. You could apply for state financial assistance, right?" Jacob directed his question at Julie.

She nodded affirmative.

Jacob truly hoped she had compassion in her heart.

"C'mon, Pete, drop the gun so we can move past this and get you on the right track. Please?"

Pete glanced from Jacob to Julie and back to Jacob. In those tense few seconds, Jacob heard Beau's voice berating him for taking a risk that could end Jacob's life when he had a little girl waiting for him at home.

Once again, Jacob couldn't walk away from people who needed help.

"Pete?" Jacob encouraged.

The kid placed the gun on the ground and took a step back, staring at the weapon as if he only now realized what he'd done.

Pete lookcd at Julie and said, "I'm sorry." He dropped to his knees and began sobbing. "I'm so sorry."

"Hands where I can see them!" Detective Harper shouted behind them.

Pete raised his hands. Harper and Deputy Taylor approached Pete and the deputy cuffed him.

"Go easy on the kid," Jacob said. "He needs help."

"Miss your old job, huh?" Harper asked Jacob.

"Very funny. We'd better call an ambulance for Brianna."

"No."

He turned to Brianna. She blinked her soft brown eyes at him. "No ambulance."

"You're okay," Jacob said, gently stroking her arm.

"Relatively speaking. Could you give me a ride to the hospital?"

"An ambulance would get you there quicker."

"No, please, I need you to take me."

Brie trusted Jacob more than she dared admit. She struggled to think of another person in her life she trusted as much. Now she was sounding crazy, and she was certainly taking up too much of this man's time. She'd tried setting her boundary, leaving the note clarifying she didn't want his help. She was trying to distance him from trouble, yet she'd dragged him right into the thick of it today with the desperate, armed student.

"How's the head?" he asked.

"A little achy. I may have hit it when I pretended to faint."

He shot her a look.

"I thought that if I acted like I needed help, it would derail the young man and perhaps trigger compassion," she said.

"Interesting theory."

"Didn't really work."

"Well, he didn't shoot anyone."

"Thanks to you. I heard how you spoke to him, with respect and compassion."

"He's in a tough spot. Seems like all the adults in his life have let him down and he lost it. I'm glad I was there to help."

"I was obviously out of my depth. The head injury probably made me think I could stop him from hurting that woman."

"He just needed someone to genuinely listen."

"How did you end up at the university in the first place?" she asked.

"I went to find Andrea Carp, to see if she knew where you'd gone."

"But I left a note—"

"I read it." He shot her a look she couldn't decipher. "Giving it to Miri was cruel."

"I didn't give it to Miri. I left it by the coffeepot in the kitchen."

"Well, she found it and was crestfallen."

"Oh, I'm so sorry."

"She's really taken to you, Brianna. You should have at least said goodbye in person."

She began to see how leaving had triggered pain of the past. For both Jacob and Miri.

"I understand."

"Do you?" he snapped.

A few minutes of silence stretched between them.

"I apologize for being curt," Jacob said. "I'm trying to move forward without carrying all the weight of the past around. Sometimes it sneaks up on me."

"The weight of the past," she said, gazing out the front window of the truck. "Gets heavier all the time, doesn't it? I wish I could toss it aside and pretend it never happened."

"Unfortunately, that doesn't work. You need to unpack it, analyze it and then let it go."

"Have you tried that?"

"I thought so, but after today I can see I've still got a lot of stuff I need to deal with."

"Like?"

He pinned her with such soulful eyes. "Aban-

donment. When you left without saying goodbye, it all came rushing back. Cassie leaving,
taking the secret about our child with her, me
missing out on the first four years of my baby
girl's life. I'm definitely not over it. I was angry
with you today."

"Are you still angry?"

"More like…hurt."

She nodded, puzzling over his comment.

"Why did you ask me to drive you to the hospital instead of going by ambulance?" he said.

"I didn't want to draw unwanted attention to
myself by pulling up in an emergency vehicle."

"Ah."

She didn't dare share the real reason—that
being around Jacob calmed her, made her feel
whole. Yet if he found out the truth about who
she truly was, and what she'd done…

"You say God forgives?" she said.

"Yes."

"Everything?"

"Why do you ask?"

"Today I found out that I'm a bad person,
Jacob."

He chuckled.

"What's so funny?" she said.

"That's not possible. You've devoted your life
to helping others, healing others."

"That's what I thought, too." She sighed. "I
accessed my work files and emails today. I dis-

covered I'm not who I think I am, who I was... Oh, it's all a massive mess."

"Slow down. What did you find out?"

"I don't want to say it out loud. Trust me, you wouldn't want to help me if you knew the truth."

"Brianna—"

"I was going to sell my research to a drug company that would bury it," she blurted out, almost as if she was trying to drive him away.

"How do you know that?"

"I found an email exchange between myself and a drug company. I'd agreed to meet with them to discuss selling my research. They would have buried it. I would have betrayed all that I had worked for, betrayed people who could have benefited from my work. For money."

He turned onto the hospital drive and parked. "Brianna, look at me."

She turned to him. He reached for her hands, and she automatically offered them.

"There's no way you'd tank your own research," he said.

"How do you know?"

"I just do." He gave her hands a gentle squeeze. "Trust yourself."

If only she could trust herself as much as it seemed Jacob trusted her.

"Now let's get you checked out by a doctor." He opened his truck door.

That's it? She'd told him what a horrible person she was and he…counseled her to trust herself? His reaction felt amazing, although slightly disconcerting.

She could get used to this kind of emotional support, but she shouldn't; it was too dangerous. Jacob deserved someone better suited for him than Brianna, like a Christian woman devoted to family and life on the ranch, not a researcher who pretended to help others when in reality she was all about herself.

Her car door opened, and Jacob offered his hand with a smile.

She took it and looked into his eyes. "I had you bring me to the hospital because I'm hoping the doctor will say it's safe to fly."

Jacob's smile faded. "Whatever you think is best."

The ER doctor was pleasant enough but wouldn't give Brianna a definitive answer about flying, or confirm if her head trauma had worsened because of her fall today. His best suggestion was to stay put for a few more days, at which time they'd schedule another CT scan.

Jacob had been polite yet distant since her proclamation that she intended to head back to Chicago as soon as possible.

Back to what? Her life as a corrupt researcher?

"For the record," Jacob said as he drove, "I think you'd be safer staying at the ranch."

"Thank you, but Andrea has offered me her guest room."

"Does she know about the threat?"

"She does. Her home has a state-of-the-art security system. If I feel vulnerable, I will contact Mr. Jenson and accept his offer of protection from his bodyguards."

"I don't trust that guy."

"Well, I don't want to keep putting you and your family at risk, Jacob."

"Why do I sense that's not the only reason you don't want to be around us, around me?"

How could this man know her so well in such a short period of time? Because her usual defenses were down.

She was vulnerable. Not a good place to be.

"For the record," he started, "it was brave of you to try and help Julie Denali in the parking lot."

"In retrospect it seems like a ridiculous move on my part."

"Never beat yourself up for trying to help someone."

"Are we close to Andrea's place?" She enjoyed his praise too much, she realized.

"According to my GPS, her driveway should be up here on the right."

As they approached Andrea's home, Brianna felt her life was spinning away from her. The only thing she could control was protecting

Jacob, which would also protect Miri and the rest of the Rogers family.

The best way to do that was detaching from Jacob sooner rather than later.

He pulled up to a call box, and Brianna gave him the code that opened the gates. Jacob parked in front of a house overlooking a valley below.

"Nice property," Jacob said.

"Her husband manages stocks, I think."

He reached for his door handle.

"I can take it from here. I'll send someone for my things tomorrow."

"I am walking you to the door and making sure you get inside, Brianna."

With a resigned nod, she got out.

As they approached the house, she felt a pang of loss at having to say goodbye to this remarkable man. It wasn't her head injury causing the pain; it was something else. She liked Jacob. She cared about him. A lot.

She pulled out her phone. "Andrea texted me the code to the house, as well."

"She's not home?"

"She's on a video meeting and said to let myself in." Brianna pressed the six-digit code, and the door unlocked with a click. She turned to Jacob. "Thank you. For everything."

He leaned forward and kissed her on the cheek. "Be safe," he said softly beside her ear.

When he stood back, their eyes caught, and

she almost forgot to breathe. She realized he was still holding her hand.

Let him go, Brianna.

She turned abruptly, breaking contact, stepped into the house and closed the door behind her.

She inhaled a deep breath and tried to calm her rapid heartbeat. Detaching from Jacob tore at her sense of stability, yet she was glad to have made the break—for his sake. Then she chided herself for sending mixed signals. One minute she had him take her to the hospital for support, the next, she was telling him she planned to leave town and didn't want his help.

Brianna lifted her chin, a bit proud of herself for releasing Jacob from his protective duties. Whatever trouble was shadowing Brianna, she'd created it, and she would deal with it.

On her own.

"I'm back here!" Andrea called.

Brianna followed the sound of her voice and entered the kitchen.

She froze at the sight of Andrea, tied to a chair, her face wet with tears.

"What…?"

"Hello, Dr. Wilkes."

Brie spun around.

And was staring at the barrel of a gun pointed at her head.

TEN

Jacob drove away from the house, eyeing his rearview mirror and wondering why he was experiencing such internal conflict. He'd told her how he felt—that she shouldn't have left the ranch without saying goodbye. He hadn't buried his anger this time and thought by being truthful the weight would lift from his heart.

It didn't.

He passed through the gates, and they closed behind him. He pulled over on the side of the road to collect his thoughts before heading back to the ranch. Something felt off, like there was still unfinished business between him and Brianna or like she didn't really want him to leave or…

Maybe he didn't want this relationship to end.

"That's crazy," he said to himself. They'd known each other days, not years.

If only it had been a few months, he would have had time to logically determine if his feelings—ones he hadn't felt since Cassie—were real or a fabrication. Was he confusing compassion for something more? Was he setting himself up for failure because on some level he believed he didn't deserve love?

"Thinking way too much," he muttered.

Brianna Wilkes had been clear: she was done with Jacob.

Then again, she wasn't thinking straight, especially if she believed she was a bad person.

He called the ranch to check on Miri. Lacey had heard about the gunman situation at the university. The Boulder Creek grapevine was in overdrive, calling Jacob a hero for intervening. Jacob didn't welcome the accolades. The attention would give Beau more reason to question Jacob's priorities.

"But you're okay?" Lacey said.

"I'm fine. The young man was in a dark place and needed to be heard. How's Miri?"

"Busy helping us serve dinner. She's a charmer."

"Don't I know it."

"You on your way back?"

"In a bit."

"And Brianna?"

He eyed the house on the other side of the gates. "She's staying with a friend in town."

"Oh. That's a shame. Cook made chocolate graham pie for dessert. She's missing out."

"Sounds delicious. See you in a bit."

Jacob ended the call. No matter how he felt about driving away, it was his only choice. Then what was with the nagging sensation at the base of his neck? He was tired, that's all. Tired from aftereffects of the sedative, tired from having to juggle so many things at once.

Tired from trying to keep Brianna safe when she kept putting herself in danger.

Another reason for concern. Was she making good, sound choices? The decision to help Julie Denali was admirable, but was it wise?

"She's an adult. Let it be." As he put the truck in Drive, the gates opened, and a silver sedan pulled out onto the road. As it passed, he saw a blonde woman in the front seat.

Brianna.

Her gaze seemed unfocused, resigned.

He instinctively followed the sedan and called Detective Harper, not letting the car out of his sight.

"Maybe I'm overreacting, but a silver car just left Andrea Carp's property, and Brianna was in the front seat. She looked…strange. Could you run the plates for me?" Jacob read the number to Detective Harper.

"Hang on," Harper said.

The car sped up, but Jacob kept following. He hoped the driver hadn't figured out she was being followed, or worse, that Brianna told the driver to lose Jacob. He wasn't some threatening stalker. He was worried about her. Where would Andrea and Brianna be going after the day she'd had?

Had Brianna convinced Andrea to take her to the airport so she could fly out of town immediately?

"Jacob?" Harper said.

"Yeah."

"Plates are coming up as a rental."

"It doesn't belong to Andrea Carp?"

"No. Hang on… What's Andrea's address?"

"Thirteen fourteen Juniper Drive."

"We got a call for suspicious activity at that address. A deputy is on the way."

"I'll follow the sedan."

"Give me your location. I'll send a deputy to intercept."

"They turned onto Mountain Trail Drive."

"On our way."

Jacob turned onto the winding road that led to the Mount Whittaker lookout, wondering why the driver had chosen this route. The sedan sped up as it approached a curve. Andrea Carp couldn't be behind the wheel, because she'd be taking the turns slower and she'd know this road was a dead end. Mountain Trail Drive led visitors to the outlook, where they could get a clear view of the beautiful valley below during the day. But why head up there at night?

Unless the plan was to make Brianna disappear.

He slowly pressed the gas pedal, not wanting to lose control of his truck. He had to be smart about this, for both himself and Brianna.

He didn't need to crowd the sedan. Jacob wouldn't lose them if he fell back a bit.

But could he lose Brianna?

Taillights disappeared around a sharp turn ahead, but Jacob didn't speed up. This road was desolate at night, and dangerous, thanks to sharp turns and limited visibility.

Jacob made the turn and felt his wheels lose their grip, the asphalt slick with the drop in temperature. The driver must not be familiar with the conditions, because he seemed to be speeding up.

"Slow down," Jacob muttered.

The driver took the next turn, locked his brakes and skidded dangerously close to the edge.

"Don't be an idiot." Jacob drifted farther behind so as not to the be the cause of the person's reckless driving.

Sirens echoed in the distance. The driver must have heard it, too, because the sedan sped up.

He called Detective Harper. "Can they shut off the sirens? It's making the perp drive faster, and I'm worried he's going to lose control of the vehicle."

"I'll take care of it."

Jacob focused on the road.

Made another sharp turn.

And spotted taillights disappear over the edge, followed by the sound of scraping metal and a crashing noise.

"No!" He pulled onto the shoulder, jumped out of the truck and scrambled to the edge.

The car's lights were blinking at him from a couple hundred feet below.

"Brianna!" he shouted.

He'd been too late.

Again.

He'd lost another person he cared about.

"Lord, why?" he ground out.

"Jacob?"

He leaned over the edge. "Brianna?"

"I'm here."

He must be losing his mind. Was guilt causing him to hear her voice even though she, too, was gone?

"I'm sorry, Brianna. I'm so sorry."

"Jacob, I'm right here."

He squinted and saw something about twenty feet below.

Blond hair. She looked up at him with terrified eyes. "Help me."

She seemed to be balancing on a ledge, clinging to tree root jutting out from the mountainside.

"Hang on a sec."

He grabbed rope from the back of his truck, opened the driver's side window and tied one end to the steering wheel. Securing the other end around his waist, he slowly lowered himself. Brianna grabbed his jacket and pulled him toward her, wrapping her arms around his waist. His boots settled on a shallow ledge. With one hand still holding the rope, he placed his other arm against behind Brianna's back.

"It's okay. You're okay," he said.

"Because you're here," she whispered.

"What happened?"

"That man… Stan from the river…"

"He was driving?"

She nodded.

"But the car's down there and you're here."

"I kicked him and jumped out when it skidded. But…but I couldn't stop myself from falling over the edge." She clung to him like she'd never let go.

"Jacob Rush!" someone called from above.

"Down here!" he answered, then whispered into Brianna's hair, "Shh, I've got you."

The next few hours were a blur.

Brianna relied on Jacob to make sensible decisions. She was too shaken to think straight.

They went back to the station to give their statements, the past few hours still feeling like a bad dream.

"Andrea Carp is grateful you acted the way you did," Detective Harper said.

Brianna snapped her attention to him. "I'm the reason someone broke into her house and threatened her at gunpoint."

"You willingly went with your abductor to protect Andrea. That was courageous."

"I'm glad you think so."

"You disagree?" Jacob challenged.

She didn't want to argue with him right now. He'd saved her—he'd put everything on the line yet again, and she didn't want to spark conflict between them.

"What else do you need from me?" she asked the detective.

"I think I have everything. I wish he gave you more details about why he kidnapped you."

"That makes two of us."

The detective stood, indicating the meeting was over. Brianna also stood and bit back a groan at a new muscle ache she sustained when she tumbled out of the car.

If could have been so much worse.

"I'll notify you when they rescue this Stan person," Detective Harper said. "Assuming he's still alive."

"I suspect he doesn't die easily," Brie said.

"You're going back to the ranch?"

"Yes," Jacob said before Brie could answer.

"I've got a plan to get her back on the property using multiple cars, so we won't be followed."

"Good. I'll contact you by phone. I won't risk coming out to the ranch in case I'm being followed."

"Thank you," Brie said.

Brie awoke the next day, but not in the Alpine Cabin.

The family had decided it was best if she stayed in the main house, because it had better security than the individual cabins. She'd wanted to argue, plead her case for independence, but she'd been utterly exhausted last night, and devastated.

By so many things.

Today was Friday, the day she was supposed to have presented her research findings and recommendations to the Viceroy Foundation board. Instead, it seemed she'd planned to sell her research for a quick buck, was being stalked by a violent man and kept putting people around her in danger.

People she cared about.

She remembered the look on Andrea's face when Brie had entered the kitchen. Andrea's cheeks had been flushed red, her eyes brimming with tears.

Brianna wanted to make it all go away. She wanted to go back to life before Montana, where she was safe, absorbed in her work and everything made sense.

"Jacob," she whispered.

No matter how much she denied it, she needed him, depended on him. Who knew what would have happened to her last night if he hadn't rescued her from the mountainside?

How could she ever repay him for his generosity, for repeatedly putting his life on the line to help her?

Frustrated by her situation, she flung the covers aside to get ready for the day. Now what would she do? She'd used the university's computers to prevent anyone from finding her location from the ranch's IP address. She couldn't go back to the university, or to town, for that matter, until she got word from the detective that they'd retrieved Stan. Yet even then, Stan may not be the only one after her. Plus, going back and forth from town to the ranch could potentially attract trouble.

The Rogers family was generous enough to offer her refuge, and in turn she would not put their lives at risk. She'd stay off the radar at the ranch until it was safe to leave town. Unfortunate, since she'd started to make progress on finding answers yesterday. Even though she'd discovered things about herself she wished she hadn't, Brie knew she was on the right track to filling in the blanks. So far everything indicated she was a fake, a phony, planning to sell her research for top dollar.

Her breath caught as she opened her blinds. The majestic mountains spanned the horizon, easing the worry pressing against her chest.

Trust yourself.

Jacob's words after she'd confessed what she'd learned: that she planned to sell her research, not share it freely with the world. He didn't judge, condemn or detach from her in any way. She'd never known anyone like Jacob. Was it his faith that caused him to be so generous and understanding?

She dressed, made her bed and took a moment before she would head to the kitchen to greet everyone. Sitting on the bed, she eyed the mountains. "Please make me worthy of their generosity," she whispered.

And wondered who she was talking to.

It didn't matter. She felt better speaking the request aloud.

To be worthy, she would make herself useful. For the next few days, she'd be the best pretend wrangler possible, helping out in the kitchen, in the barn, maybe even on trail rides. Then she'd leave it all behind, taking with her the memory of an amazingly kind family.

And an amazing, caring man, gentle father and friend named Jacob Rush.

Really, Brie? Just a friend?

Someone tapped softly at her bedroom door. Brianna opened it to Miri, who was looking up at her with her father's green eyes. Miri clutched her owl in one hand and a small glass bottle in the other.

"Good morning," Brianna said.

Miri thrust the purple bottle at Brianna.

"What's this?"

"You rub it here." The little girl pressed two fingers to her own temple. "It helps your headache."

Brianna inspected the bottle of lavender essential oil. "Thank you, Miri."

"Nanna made chocolate chip banana waffles." Miri reached for Brie's hand.

The connection warmed Brie's heart. She shut the bedroom door and let the child lead her downstairs, a tangle of emotion rising in Brie's chest.

"I still don't understand why you brought her back here," Beau said.

"You would understand if you'd been at the family meeting last night," Beau's mother said.

It was a good thing Lacey had responded, because Jacob wasn't in the mood to argue with Beau. Jacob had gotten maybe five hours of sleep, reliving the moment when he'd scrambled to the edge of the road and thought Brianna dead, over and over again.

She's safe, he kept repeating to himself. Still, he got up a few times to patrol the house, to make sure everyone was safe and secure.

That Miri and Brianna were safe.

"Dad, you're good with this?" Beau asked his father, who was loading the dishwasher.

Bill stopped, turned off the water and looked at his son. "'My little children, let us not love in word or in tongue, but in deed and in truth.' It's the right thing to do, Beau, to help a young woman who's in trouble. You, of all people, know that, son."

Beau clenched his jaw and left the kitchen.

Jacob looked at Miri's grandpa and nodded his thanks. Bill went back to finishing the dishes.

"Miri seems happy that Brianna is back," Lacey said.

"She certainly does."

"It's going to be hard on her when Brianna leaves."

Jacob nodded. What could he say? It was going to be hard on both of them.

Brianna and Miri entered the kitchen, Miri leading Brianna by the hand. Oh man, this wasn't going to be hard; it was going to be devastating.

"Good morning," Brianna said.

"How did you sleep?" Lacey asked. "Did the family make too much noise this morning?"

"I slept surprisingly well, thanks." She pulled out her phone and frowned.

"What's wrong?" Jacob said.

"A text from Detective Harper. Apparently my kidnapper was not in the vehicle when they retrieved it."

"That's unfortunate," Lacey said.

Then it was a good thing Jacob was up last night patrolling. Brianna's eyes met his, and he wanted to ease her worried frown. Before he could offer a kind touch or maybe even a hug, Miri stepped in front of him.

"I gave her the oil for her headache, Papa Jay. Gramps, where are the waffles for Miss Brianna?"

"Top shelf of the fridge, kiddo."

Miri released Brianna and went to get Brianna's breakfast, even taking it to the microwave so her grandfather could heat it up. Jacob noticed Brianna shove her hands into her fleece pockets as if suddenly chilled.

"Lacey and Bill?" Brianna said.

Bill turned, wiping his hands on a towel.

"I don't know how to thank you for allowing me to return to the ranch. I left in order to protect you." She turned to Jacob. "And Jacob, I might not be alive but for your kindness and generosity."

She went to him and gave him a hug. He hadn't expected that and didn't return the gesture at first. It was then he realized he was using distancing skills honed as a counselor to keep the boundaries clear between him and Brianna. That's why he didn't automatically hug her back.

Then something broke inside, and he wrapped his arms around her. The moment felt surreal, almost like a dream. This wasn't a hug of desperation like yesterday on the mountain ledge. This was something different, much deeper.

Miri giggled, shattering the moment. Brianna released him.

"Why don't you have a seat and eat your breakfast, Brianna?" Lacey said, shooting Jacob a look.

She slid onto a kitchen bar stool, and Bill handed her a fork. "Please know it's our pleasure to provide you with a safe haven until you sort things out. We get as much out of helping you as you do, if not more. Well, I'm headed out to wrestle the morning trail ride away from my bossy son. Jacob, I was hoping you could do maintenance on the barn today?"

"Will do, sir."

"What would you like me to do today?" Brianna asked.

"Rest," Jacob said.

Brianna put down her fork and addressed Lacey and Bill. "For however long I'm here, I need to feel useful. It will distract me from worrying myself into a stressful sinkhole."

"Stressful sinkhole," Lacey repeated. "Someone should share that expression with Beau."

"Come on, Miss Owl." Bill extended his hand to Miri. "Let's get you to Little Wrangler's Club."

"Not Miss Owl, just Owl," Miri corrected. She hopped off her stool, gave Brianna a hug and left with her grandfather.

Lacey slid her mug of coffee onto the kitchen island and sat across from Brianna. "We admire your courage, Brianna. Jacob told us you went with that man last night to protect your friend."

"To think what would have happened if Jacob hadn't followed me."

"It's a good thing I was still there. Which reminds me, can I see your phone?"

She handed it to him without hesitation.

"If you don't mind, I'm sharing my location and vice versa, in case I'm not around next time," he said.

"Probably a good idea." She stabbed her waffle with her fork. "With Stan on the loose, I can't rationalize going back to the university to use their computers. I was making progress yesterday, digging into my files, finding answers. It made me feel like I was fighting my own battles instead of being a victim needing constant rescue."

"Then keep digging," Lacey said. "Use the computer in our den."

Jacob handed her back the phone.

"I won't risk someone tracing the IP address to the ranch," Brianna said.

"What about borrowing a notebook computer from the university?" Jacob suggested.

"I was planning to call Andrea and check on how she's doing."

"Good. See if you can borrow a laptop, and if not, I'll look into a VPN service for the ranch's computer. I'd better get going on the maintenance work. See you at lunch." He turned to leave.

"Jacob?"

He hesitated. If she hugged him again, he might lose it and confess how he really felt—about her, about their impossible relationship, about wanting her to stay in Montana.

He turned to her.

"Thanks again," she said. "For everything."

He nodded and got out of there before *he* pulled *her* into a hug. And didn't let go.

As Brianna finished breakfast, Lacey kept her company and asked questions about Brie's work. Lacey seemed impressed by Brie's vision and determination, and said she was honored to offer such an "admirable woman" a safe haven.

Apparently Brie wasn't the first woman who'd sought refuge at the Boulder Creek Ranch. The family didn't talk about it because they didn't boast about their good deeds. But Lacey thought it important to tell Brianna about Harriet Adams, a young woman caught in an abusive tug-of-war between her father and her boyfriend. Harriet wouldn't file assault charges against either man because on some level she loved them both and had been raised to think physical abuse was a normal part of a male-female relationship; hence, she'd planned to marry her abusive boyfriend.

"Harriet was my hairdresser," Lacey said. "At one of my appointments, I noticed bruising on her arms and neck. When I asked her about it, she said she got them wrestling with her dog. She owned a shih tzu. When I asked around town, it became clear she needed help." Lacey sighed. "The poor girl had such low self-esteem. The men in her life convinced her she was stupid, worthless and couldn't function without them. Can you believe anyone would talk that way to someone they said they loved?"

"That's not love," Brie said, thinking about her own childhood experience as well.

"I couldn't sit by and do nothing. So, the Rogers family committed to helping Harriet. First, we housed her at the ranch under an assumed name. Once we got the paperwork in order and raised a little extra money, we helped her quietly leave town with her dog. She sent her father and her boyfriend letters explaining she'd gone to live with her aunt in Florida. We worried they'd go in search of her, but it didn't matter. She wasn't really at her aunt's." Lacey winked.

"How did the men react?" Brianna asked.

"Her father blamed the boyfriend and vice

versa. It culminated with a public brawl. The boyfriend fell and cracked his head open. Harriet's father was sentenced to six years in prison for assault, and the boyfriend will be in a rehab center for life. He'll never be able to function on his own. So sad."

"And Harriet?"

"She's doing quite well. Legally changed her name and earned a college degree. She's living in Colorado, working in law enforcement, of all things. My point is, the Rogers family doesn't shy away from conflict if someone needs help."

"Beau isn't too happy with me being here."

"It's probably triggering painful memories. I think he secretly wanted Harriet to stay with us indefinitely. He and Harriet became quite close when she was here. That was more than ten years ago. At some point Beau has to let go of things—people, like Harriet and Cassie."

"Cassie?"

"He was her big brother. On some level he blames himself for her death. He's so…angry. I pray for my boy every night that the Lord will soften his heart or that perhaps he'll find a good counselor. I thought Jacob could help. He's a kind man and knows how to ask the right questions."

"But he hasn't?"

"Oh, he's tried. Unfortunately, Jacob represents more loss for Beau. Before Jacob came to live with us, Beau was the closest thing Miri had to a father. When Jacob showed up, it felt like Beau had lost Miri, too, which of course he hadn't. She still adores him."

"That's why she calls him Papa Beau," Brie said.

"Like I said, I pray every night. Sometimes that's the only thing you can do."

Brianna nodded, remembering how she'd sort of prayed that she'd be worthy of this family's generosity.

"Anyway, we're ready and able to protect you from the people trying to derail your good work," Lacey said.

"Thank you. You, your whole family, is amazing."

"We're instruments of God." Lacey glanced at her watch. "I need to check on the Little Wrangler's Club. You're welcome to help out there until you get your computer situation figured out. But take your time finishing breakfast."

"Thanks, it's delicious."

"I'm glad you think so." Lacey grabbed her jacket and headed out, leaving Brie alone in the kitchen.

It was so quiet, peaceful, and it gave Brie a moment to process the story Lacey had shared about Harriet Adams. Such remarkable people. Jacob was fortunate to have ended up with this family even if tragedy had brought him to Boulder Creek. He'd made a life for himself among the Rogers clan, raising his child in a nurturing, loving environment with family all around. What Brie wouldn't have given for that kind of upbringing.

She was torn being back here, embracing the feeling of safety while fighting the guilt for putting the family in danger. Yet Lacey made it clear they knew the risks. Such a generous woman who freely shared love and compassion, even with a virtual stranger like Brie.

She walked her empty plate over to the sink. Glancing out the window, Brie spotted Jacob crossing the property carrying a tool belt.

For half a second she wondered what it would be like to commit her life to a man like Jacob, live on a ranch surrounded by a loving family, running the business, raising a family of her own.

"Everything okay?" Rose joined Brie at the sink and also looked out the window. "Oh." Rose quirked an eyebrow. "Does he know?"

Brie snapped her attention to Rose. "No, no. It's not like that. He's a close friend, that's all."

"That's what I used to say about T.J.—I mean, Detective Harper."

"Used to?"

"We're figuring it out, I think, maybe, possibly. There's a lot of baggage there." She shrugged. "But life's too short not to be brutally honest, even if you encounter bumps along the way."

"I like your attitude."

"Thanks. I've been working on it." Rose poured a cup of coffee. "What's on your schedule today?"

"Get access to a computer that won't lead my enemies back to the ranch. My enemies. I can't even believe I am saying that."

"How about using my laptop? I have a VPN service. Had it installed when I went into business for myself."

"I don't understand. Aren't you part of the ranch business?"

"I help out, but I mainly run my own business training dogs, pet sitting, that sort of thing. There are a lot of wealthy folks in Montana who like to travel without their pets, and when they're home, they like the dogs to behave. I'll get my laptop from the car and meet you in the den."

"Thank you very much."

Brie pulled out her temporary cell phone and paused before calling Andrea. Brie felt guilty that she'd put the woman in danger last night.

"You did not threaten her with a gun," she said, stepping off the guilt train. What had Lacey said? She admired Brie's courage when she'd sacrificed her own safety for Andrea's.

Brie needed to stop taking responsibility for everyone else's behavior and focus on her own, even if that meant she'd have to admit betraying herself and her research team for money. Money had to be her motivation, right? That didn't feel right, either. She didn't lack for money. She lived a comfortable if not extravagant life.

She shoved aside her puzzlement and called Andrea, but it went into voice mail. "Andrea, it's Brianna Wilkes. I'm so sorry about what happened last night. I wanted to let you know I'm okay and I hope you are, too. Again, please forgive me for involving you in this mess. Thank you."

Brie wandered down the hall to the den. If she could safely use Rose's computer, she would continue her investigation and narrow down who was after her and why.

One person she hadn't conferred with recently was Douglas. Again, shame kept her from having that conversation. Her research partner would be crushed to know she was a fake, a phony.

Jacob believed in her. Why couldn't she believe in herself?

Rose joined her in the den and placed the laptop on the desk. Something caught her attention outside. "Oh, no."

Brie looked out the window and saw Oscar the dog chasing a goat.

"The problem with this mixed breed is sometimes the neurotic border collie genes dominate the chill golden retriever genes. I'd better get him before he chases Ginger the goat up the mountain."

Rose left, and Brie opened the laptop. First,

she should call Douglas. Better yet, she could do a video chat. That way she could read his expression when she questioned him about potentially selling the research. Perhaps he had information that could clear this up.

She texted Douglas, alerting him to check his email for a video chat link. He responded that he was in a meeting but would be finished in twenty minutes. She spent the time checking emails until her phone beeped with a text that he was available. She opened the chat to Douglas's intense expression.

"Brianna, what's wrong?"

"I was nearly kidnapped again last night."

"What?" he said, shocked.

"I don't know what's going on, but I could use your help."

"What do you need?"

"I've been looking through emails, trying to piece together who would want to threaten me about our project. I found something indicating we planned to sell our research instead of publishing the findings."

He leaned back in his chair. "Sell our research?"

"Yes, but I don't understand why we would do that."

"Neither do I. We have completed the study and are ready to publish. Who would we sell to? Not a pharmaceutical company—they'd bury it."

"I realize it doesn't make sense, but neither does someone wanting to kidnap me for our research."

"Give me the weekly access code and I'll do some digging."

"You don't have it?"

"You change it every Tuesday and didn't share it before you left. Don't you remember?"

Brianna didn't immediately respond. Something was bothering her.

"Brianna? You don't remember the code?"

"I'm not sure I'm comfortable sharing it over the phone."

A hooded man stepped up behind Douglas.

"Douglas, look out!"

An arm wrapped around his neck and pulled him backward, out of sight. Brianna jumped to her feet. "Douglas!"

Scuffling and crashing sounds echoed through the laptop. Then, silence.

She could barely breathe past the panic tightening her chest. Something covered the camera lens in a black haze.

"Dr. Wilkes," a voice said. "Give me the access code or your Montana friend is next."

ELEVEN

Her Montana friend?

Jacob.

Jacob was in danger.

Brie rushed out of the house.

On some level she knew one man couldn't be in two places at once. Douglas's attacker couldn't get to Jacob.

But one of his associates could.

They hadn't found Stan's body. He was still out there, looking for her, threatening people she cared about.

Had he discovered her location? She'd been foolish to come back here. Of course her attacker knew she'd hidden here before!

She raced toward the barn, wishing she had some kind of weapon to defend herself and Jacob. She hadn't intended to put the family at risk again. She was supposed to be safe here; everyone was supposed to be okay.

Douglas was definitely not okay.

She called Detective Harper. "My research partner in Chicago… Douglas West, he's been assaulted, maybe killed. Roundtree Labs, One North Wacker Drive. Call the Chicago police!"

"Slow down."

"The man said my Montana friend was next. That has to be Jacob. Or what if it's Andrea?"

"I'll get in touch with Mrs. Carp."

"I have to find Jacob!"

"Dr. Wilkes—"

Pocketing her phone, she raced into the barn and searched frantically for a weapon. She grabbed a pitchfork, but didn't call Jacob's name for fear she'd alert a would-be attacker to her presence.

She slowly made her way from stall to stall holding the pitchfork in front of her. A grunting sound drew her attention to the other end of the barn. Could she really stab a man?

If it meant defending Jacob? Yes, she could.

With slow and measured steps, she headed through the barn toward the opposite exit. She whipped around and aimed the pitchfork…

At Jacob, who lay on the ground.

She stood protectively over him and scanned the area. "Where is he?"

"Who?"

"The man who did this?"

"You're looking at him." He sat up and coughed.

"What do you mean?"

He pointed up above at a hay loft opening. "Embarrassed to say I lost my balance and fell."

She dropped the pitchfork and hugged him, tight.

"You really need to stop doing that," he said.

She broke the hug. "Am I hurting you?"

"No, you're not hurting me, not in the way you think. At least not yet."

In that moment she knew what he was saying. He felt it, too, the connection between them, and he'd be upset when she left Montana.

"What's going on?" he said.

"My research partner, Douglas—we were on a video chat and someone attacked him and… and I think he's dead."

"Whoa, there." This time he pulled her into a hug. "Did you notify the police?"

"I called Detective Harper. Gave him details."

"That's all you can do for now."

"It's not enough." She swiped tears off her cheeks. Tears. She hadn't remembered crying since…since her mother died. She learned early on that tears gave her emotionally abusive aunt power over Brie. Brie had turned off her ability to cry, to show emotion of any kind. It was the best way to protect herself.

Yet she was crying in front of Jacob.

Because she feared Douglas had been killed?

Yes, but also because she felt utterly devastated at the thought of Jacob being hurt.

Of losing him.

"What can I do to help?" Jacob said.

"Help?"

"Yes, help you figure out what's going on. The sooner you figure it out, the sooner you can go back to living a normal life."

"Normal. I don't even know what that means anymore. For that matter, I don't even know who I am."

He got to his feet and groaned, pressing his hand against his lower back. "Keep this between us, would you?"

"The attack on Douglas?"

"No, my clumsiness. I *am* sorry about your research partner."

"The man who attacked him said you were next."

"He knows my name?"

"No, he said my 'Montana friend.'"

"And you thought he was here?"

"Or one of his associates, like Stan."

"Stan was probably thrown from the car and they haven't found his body yet."

"Or he's close by and someone in the Rogers family will be hurt because of me. Oh, I should have found a way to get back to the lab in Chicago. That's where I belong, not out here."

"If you were back at the lab, you would have also been hurt. You're exactly where you belong.

You've notified authorities about Douglas's danger. You can't do more than that right now."

"It doesn't feel right. I'm constantly stressed, which is probably going to trigger some kind of autoimmune response in my own body, yet I act like an expert on managing autoimmune attacks. I'm a fake, a real phony."

He looked into her eyes. "No, you're human. You're responding as anyone would in your situation. Your life's been threatened multiple times, people you care about are being hurt and you haven't a clue why. Our first reaction is to click into defensive mode. Makes complete sense. But what will you do next, stay stressed and reactive to everything or find the inner strength to help you find peace, which will lead you out of this?"

"I'm not sure I know how to find peace."

"I think you do. Isn't that what you've been researching? How to work with your body to stop it from attacking itself?"

"Well, yes, but—"

"Start there. What tools were you studying?"

"Productive sleep, healthy nutrition, breath work."

"Breath work, you mentioned that before. What else?"

"Being out in nature."

He motioned to their surroundings. "Check. And?"

"A sense of community."

"Welcome to the Rogers family." He winked. "Next?"

"Practicing gratitude. We'd better skip that one."

"Actually, let's start there." He took her hand and led her to a nearby wooden bench. "One of the things I've learned is that when you're in the moment, not thinking about what happened yesterday or what's going to happen next week, it's easier to focus on the good things surrounding you. Right now, in this moment, I'm breathing in fresh, mountain air in a gorgeous place, sitting beside a lovely woman. I am grateful for all those things. Your turn."

"I'm grateful for... I don't know, this is awkward. I'm usually the one conducting the experiments, not participating in them."

He took her hand, and warmth drifted up her arm. "Right here. Right now," he said. "What are you grateful for? Close your eyes if you need to."

She closed her eyes, fighting the voice in her head telling her this was silly, that Brie was being silly.

It was her aunt's voice. And it was about time she stopped listening.

She took a deep breath and opened her eyes. "I am grateful for the sound of the creek, the smell of horses and sunshine. I am grateful you were not attacked today. I'm... I'm grateful to be here with you."

"Likewise." He squeezed her hand and bowed his head. Was he praying?

A few seconds later, he looked up. "How are you feeling?"

"A little better."

"I'm no researcher, but may I suggest you add something to your personal stress-reduction list?"

"Like what?"

"Forgiveness."

She couldn't help but make a face of displeasure.

"Hang in there with me, Brianna. I believe if we cling to these toxic feelings longer than we should, they become part of our DNA and affect our health, our decision-making ability. We can't scrape them off unless we intentionally work at it. I've been working at it for a few years now, mostly with the help of God, which probably makes you uncomfortable, but—"

"It's just, I wasn't raised knowing any kind of god or supreme being. I was taught that everything that happened to me in life was my own fault."

"There's so much we don't understand, Brianna."

"From a scientist's perspective, I agree with that statement."

"For me that's where God comes in. He helps me feel stable and centered when I am surrounded by chaos. You don't have to use God as your conduit to forgiveness. I do because it helps. He's a master at it. He forgives us all."

She considered his words. "And forgiving, you think that helps reduce stress?"

"Absolutely. I want you to think about people in your life you need to forgive."

She nodded, but in truth she was starting to feel anxious. Her aunt was the first person who popped into her mind. Then her father, for starting a new family and forgetting about Brie, and Brie's mother for intentionally running her car into a tree. Then there was Brie's sister, who started off the chain of tragic events when she died. Brie shook her head.

"What?" Jacob said.

"I'm ashamed of myself."

"Why?"

"I'm angry with my sister for dying. How ridiculous is that?"

"That's your ten-year-old self talking. It's not ridiculous, it's understandable. Take a few deep breaths and forgive your sister, and anyone else who you feel has wronged you."

"What if I can't?"

"You can. I have faith in you. The resentment you have for them won't disappear right away, but if you take the time to work at it, your stress will loosen up as you willingly let the resentment go."

They spent a few minutes breathing in and out, silently practicing forgiveness. As an adult she was able to logically release the resentment she'd been holding on to, but the child within her struggled desperately to cling to the sadness. He was right; it had become a part of her.

A few minutes later, she heard him say, "Amen."

"You must have been really good at your job," she said.

"Thanks, but the forgiveness piece didn't come until after I'd left my job in Detroit."

"When you learned about Miri."

"Yep. Are you feeling better?"

"A little calmer. I think I know what to do next."

"What?"

"I need to put an end to my vulnerable position and figure out who's after me, even if it means I learn things about myself I won't like."

"Not to worry." He squeezed her hand. "Remember, even if you find it hard to forgive yourself, He forgives."

Jacob spent the rest of the day going down the list of fixes on the barn and the night pasture fence as Brianna spent her time investigating who might be after her. Jacob would text her every few hours to check in. Detective Harper learned her research partner had been taken to the hospital with only minor injuries. Brianna texted Jacob she added that to her gratitude list, along with the news that Andrea Carp was safe and had hired an off-duty sheriff's deputy as a temporary bodyguard.

Lacey kept an eye on Brianna when she could, and reported to Jacob that Miri couldn't stay away from the fascinating woman who seemed to know everything about owls.

They had just served the guests their final dinner of the week when Jacob realized Brie wasn't among the group.

"Anyone seen Brianna?" he said.

"You're as bad as your daughter," Beau muttered.

"I think she's in the den," Lacey offered. "You two want to eat in there?"

Jacob eyed the kids' table, where Miri was telling a story to a little girl seated next to her.

"I'll keep an eye on Miri," Lacey said.

"Great, thanks."

Lacey helped him fix two plates of chicken, green beans and mashed potatoes. He carried them down the hall and overheard Brianna's voice echo from the open door to the den.

"I don't understand. It's not our fault... We've made great progress... I understand, but... How long?"

Jacob joined her in the den. Brianna, eyes closed, sat behind the desk, pressing two fingers against her forehead. He slid the food onto the desk and sat in the chair across from her.

"Let's set up a meeting when I return. I should be cleared to fly early week... Thank you."

She ended the call and looked at him. "They've shut down the lab."

"Because of the attack on your partner?"

"That, and they're opening an investigation on me. They're questioning my integrity, the integrity of our study," she said. "The Viceroy Foundation received correspondence from a whistleblower claiming I planned to present findings to the board that our solutions were not statistically significant, then turn around and sell that very research to a drug company for millions of dollars. As I said before, the only reason a drug company would want our research is if it was proven effective, thereby threatening their bottom line. None of this makes sense."

"Brianna, what do you believe to be true?"

"I don't know. I've been confused since the head injury and—"

"In your heart, Brianna. What does your heart tell you?"

She blinked her brown eyes at him. "I would not betray all that I believe in. I am a woman of integrity."

"Then you are, no matter what anyone else says or what they claim they know—"

"But I found emails—"

"Call them, talk to them."

"Who?"

"The people you've supposedly been in touch with about selling the research. Do more digging, prove yourself innocent of any wrongdoing, because I know you are."

She used relaxation techniques she and Jacob had practiced to help her sleep and awoke the next morning feeling grounded. She started off the day making calls to dig further into the mystery emails, but she mostly got voice mail due to it being the weekend.

It still bothered her that she didn't remember sending the emails, perhaps because of the head injury. She wondered how long it would take for the swelling to go down and for her cognitive function to return to normal.

Shoving her trepidation aside, she chose to help the family say goodbye to this week's guests. New guests were arriving on Monday, so the family and crew would spend Saturday and Sunday afternoon prepping for the new group. Sunday morning would be reserved for church services. Brianna considered going, wondering if the quiet time with God might ease her worry and help her find clarity. What was she missing about her current situation?

Once the guests had packed up and left, she ate lunch and returned to the den for privacy.

She wanted to check on Douglas and break the bad news about the lab in case he hadn't been notified.

Before she could phone her partner, Andrea called.

"Thank you so much for calling me back," Brie said. "How arc you?"

"I'm fine. Tougher than I look, actually. How are you holding up?"

"The threats keep coming. They broke into my lab back in Chicago."

"You must be close to something big for them to come after you like this."

"I suppose. But it might be moot, since I'm under investigation." She gave a quick summary of what was happening.

"I'm confident you'll clear your name," Andrea offered.

"It amazes me how my new friends in Montana seem to have more faith in me than my own foundation."

"They have no choice. They're following protocol. I consider myself a pretty good judge of character and I don't see you doing anything corrupt."

"I appreciate that."

"You're welcome. And I'm serious about working with you again in the future."

"Even after what happened? "

"It wasn't your fault."

"Thanks. Be safe."

"You, too."

Brie ended the call and prepared herself for the next one with Douglas. She got his voice mail and hung up, not wanting to leave a message about something as important as their lab closing.

He called back moments later.

"Brianna? You didn't leave a message."

"I'm sorry. I wanted to speak with you, not leave a message. How are you feeling?"

"A little sore but nothing serious. I gave police a full statement. Unfortunately, they couldn't identify the attacker from security video. I don't think it was random, Brianna. He was after something very specific."

"Yes, he demanded the weekly access code."

"What? You didn't—"

"No, I didn't give it to him."

"Because you couldn't remember?"

"Because I'm protecting our work."

"Give it to me and—"

"No, you need to rest. I'm safe for now. I'll do some more digging and figure out who's behind all this."

Miri ran into the den and launched herself into Brie's lap. "Miri, I'm on the phone, sweetie."

The little girl giggled.

"Who's Miri?" Douglas asked.

"A little wrangler with an inquisitive nature."

Brie tickled Miri's ribs and shooed her out of the room. "Sorry about that. I'm glad you're okay, Douglas. Did someone from Viceroy contact you?"

"About…?"

She took a deep breath. "They're shutting down the lab until further notice."

"That's not right," he said in an indignant tone.

"They received a whistleblower report. I'm under investigation for supposedly misrepresenting our findings."

"Brianna, that's ridiculous."

"I know. I should be able to clear everything up by the time I return."

"When will that be?"

"I'm hoping I'll be okayed to fly early next week."

"There's no time to waste. We need to brainstorm, figure out how to save your reputation—the lab's reputation. I'll fly out tomorrow and meet you in Boulder Creek."

"I appreciate the thought, but you need to take care of yourself."

"We're a team, Brianna. Isn't that why you went to Montana? To speak about working as a team?"

"Yes, but—"

"I've dedicated my career to the autoimmune project under your staunch vision. I won't abandon you to fight this alone. I'll text you my flight information and lodging."

"Douglas—"

"It's appropriate to accept help, Brianna. I'll see you tomorrow."

The call ended, and Brianna sighed. He was right; it was about time she learned to graciously accept help instead of fighting to do everything solo.

That was why the guest ranch was so successful—everyone had a role to play and worked as a team to keep the place running smoothly.

Someone tapped on the door.

"Yes?"

Jacob entered. "Dinner's ready. Bill's famous brisket and corn on the cob."

"Great, thanks."

"What's goin' on?" he said, studying her.

"I spoke with my research partner. He's determined to come to Montana tomorrow to help clear my name so we can get the lab up and running again."

"Sounds like a supportive guy."

"Yes."

"I hear a *but*."

"I don't like involving any more people than I already have. It's bad enough that the Rogers family has been dragged into this."

"Nobody dragged them into anything. They're

adults who willingly made the decision to support you."

"But why?"

"That's what people do."

"Not the people in my life."

He extended his hand. "How about you leave the past behind for a few hours and join me, us, for dinner? Just the family. Wranglers have the night off."

She took his hand and appreciated the sincerity of his green eyes. "I've never known anyone like you, Jacob."

"I'll take that as a compliment." He led her down the hallway to the dining room, where everyone was seated.

They said a prayer of thanks for their meal and began passing food dishes. Miri shifted closer to Brie and smiled. Beau and his father discussed plans for a new trail ride, and Rose discussed her challenges training Oscar for search-and-rescue missions.

"The only thing that dog can find is a biscuit," Beau said, passing the bowl of corn.

"Don't listen to him, Oscar," Rose said. "He's jealous that you're more handsome than he is."

"Looks aren't everything," Beau countered. "Especially if he can't catch scent."

"Oscar's smart. I need to figure out how to tap into that intelligence."

"He's a dog, Rose," Beau said.

"And smarter than most people I know, Beau-Beau."

"Don't call me that."

"Or what?"

"Children, children," Lacey said, smiling at Brie. "Sorry about my ill-mannered adult children acting like twelve-year-olds."

After an hour of conversation, Brie found herself still enjoying the teasing banter shared between family members.

For a brief moment, this felt normal—better than normal.

Brie felt whole.

Until sudden gunfire made her gasp.

TWELVE

Grabbing Miri with one hand and Brianna with the other, Jacob pulled them both down to the floor beside him. Oscar burst into a round of frantic barks.

"Oscar, quiet," Rose said.

"Papa Jay! Papa Beau!" Miri cried.

"Beau, get the lights," Bill ordered.

Jacob kept his eyes trained on Miri, but he wasn't letting go of Brianna. "Miri, honey, you're okay."

She buried her face against his chest, whimpering. He turned to Brianna. She put up a brave front, but he read fear in her eyes. Jacob heard Beau scramble across the room. Then Jacob looked beneath the long, wooden dining table and saw Lacey, who seemed more perturbed than scared.

Beau shut the lights off.

"Everyone okay?" Bill asked.

"Me, Miri and Brianna are okay," Jacob said.

"I am *not* okay," Miri announced. "That was loud!"

"What on earth...?" Beau said as he peered out the window. "The horses are out of the barn."

"Beau, stay put," Bill ordered.

"Who knows where they'll end up!" He rushed out the back door, slamming it behind him.

"That kid," Bill muttered.

"Yes, Emergency, this is Lacey Rogers at Boulder Creek Ranch. I'd like to report gunfire. Two shots, I think?"

"I counted three," Brie suddenly said.

Jacob glanced at her. From the reflection of a full moon he could tell she wouldn't make eye contact. She was focused on Miri, who clung to Jacob.

"Three shots. Sounds good. Thank you. They're sending a deputy," Lacey said to the group. "It could be hunters or someone doing target practice."

"At night?" Rose shot back.

"A drunk kid doing target practice?" Lacey tried again.

Bill went to the window.

"You see Beau?" Lacey said.

"No. Stubborn kid. Always jumping into hot water before he takes the temperature. Wait, there he is. And he's got four wranglers with him. I'm going out. The rest of you stay put."

"I'm coming." Jacob peeled Miri off him. "Honey, go see Nanna. I've gotta help Gramps."

Instead, she flung herself at Brianna, who held her close.

"Are you—"

"It's fine," Brianna said to him.

Jacob joined Bill as he went outside to investigate. The Rogers family seemed to process hearing random gunshots in stride. But Jacob struggled to bury the trauma that haunted his dreams.

As they approached the barn, Bill nodded at Jacob. "You all right, son?"

"Yes, sir."

"Over here!" Beau called.

Bill and Jacob caught up with Beau and the four wranglers by the watering trough, where a ranch truck was banked in a ditch.

"Wranglers were coming back from town and spotted a sedan speeding up the drive," Beau said. "Ran them off the road."

"The guy was crazy, like he was trying to hit us," Chip said.

"He was even waving a gun!" Heidi offered.

"Let's get the horses," Beau ordered.

Jacob took a few steps, and Beau put out his hand. "Not you, Detroit. Stay back and take care of your daughter."

Jacob fumed. He was a part of this team, yet he was being benched. Bill placed a hand on his shoulder. "He's right. She needs you more than we do."

When Jacob returned to the house, he was surprised to find Miri completely distracted by her aunt.

"Papa Jay! Oscar and Auntie Rose are going to help me find owls," Miri said.

"Awesome, kiddo."

It amazed him how a child's moods could swing from frightened to joyful in mere minutes.

Miri looked up at her aunt. "How do you know Oscar can find an owl?"

"Well, I'm training him to find people who are lost in the mountains. I don't see why I couldn't train him to find owls by sound. What kind of sound do they make again?"

"Hoot, hoot."

"Let's hide in the house and make that sound. When he finds us, he'll get a treat." Rose looked at Jacob. "Mom and Brianna are in the kitchen."

Jacob went into the candlelit kitchen, where Lacey was washing dishes as if nothing had just happened, as if their lives hadn't been threatened by random gunfire.

These people were amazing.

"The guy took off, so we can turn the lights back on," Jacob said.

"Not in here, Papa Jay!" Miri called from the other room. "Oscar needs to find the owl at night!"

He switched the lights on in the kitchen. Brianna was pale and her gaze distant.

"We're safe," he said.

Clenching her jaw, Brianna hugged herself. Rose joined them.

Miri's voice echoed from the dining room as she argued with Oscar. "Sniff, Oscar, sniff. No, not sit. Auntie Rose!"

"Be right there, honey! She's one resilient kid," she said to Lacey, Brie and Jacob. "Hey, I've got an idea. How about I bring Miri back to my place for a sleepover?"

"You sure, Rose?" Jacob said.

"We're due for much-needed auntie-niece time."

"That's probably a good idea," Lacey agreed. "Never thought I'd be glad you had your own place instead of moving back to the ranch."

Miri entered the kitchen holding a doggie treat high in the air with Oscar trailing close. "Hoot, hoot," she said to Oscar.

"Miri, honey, go help Aunt Rose pack some of your things for a sleepover," Lacey said.

"Is Papa Jay coming?"

"Not this time, sweetheart," Jacob said.

Miri's face scrunched as if she was about to burst into tears. Jacob knelt so he'd be face-to-face with her. "It's for one night. You girls will have fun. I'll see you tomorrow."

"Promise?"

"Absolutely."

"C'mon, honey." Rose took her hand and led her out of the kitchen.

Jacob agreed that this was the best course of action. Rose lived in a secure building in the same complex as Detective Harper and two other deputies. His daughter would be safe there, especially now since Brianna's location had been discovered by her enemies, who might potentially return to the ranch.

"I should go, not Miri," Brianna said.

"We're not going to cast you out," Lacey said.

Jacob was glad the comment came from the matriarch of the family.

"This is my fault." Brianna pinned Jacob with desperate brown eyes. "Why couldn't you let me go?"

Half an hour later, anger and frustration clenched Brie's gut. That and more.

Utter sadness.

"I miss you, Papa Jay! I miss you!" Miri cried.

She hadn't even left yet and each time the child pleaded or whimpered, it felt like a knife was being plunged into Brie's heart.

She'd caused that. Her work, meant to help and potentially heal, was separating a little girl from her father. Brie should leave, but she couldn't if she wanted to remain safe, and yet by staying she was putting other people at risk.

People she cared deeply about.

Someone tapped on her bedroom door. "Come in."

It cracked open, and Jacob peered inside. "Lacey is making hot fudge sundaes."

Brie shook her head. "I am so sorry."

"You don't like hot fudge sundaes?"

"You know what I meant."

"You have nothing to be sorry about."

"I heard Miri. It's my fault she's so upset. If I wasn't here—"

"It's good for Miri to spend time with her aunt."

"You sent her away because I brought trouble to the ranch."

He stepped into her room and tipped her chin to look into his eyes. "You did not *intentionally* bring trouble here, Brianna." He smiled, and she nodded her agreement.

As he turned to leave, she got a text message. Probably from Douglas with his flight information.

She looked at her phone. It was an image of Miri's adorable face with a text.

Meet me tomorrow or I'm coming for the kid.

Panic shot to her core.

"You coming?" Jacob asked.

She looked at him. Looked at this man who'd given her so much.

And yet Brie could be responsible for destroying his life if she made the wrong choice.

"In a minute," she recovered. "I need to take care of something."

He narrowed his eyes as if discerning the sincerity of her words. She knew what she had to do to protect him, to protect his child.

"I won't be long." She forced a smile through the maelstrom of dread swirling in her body.

"Nuts and whipped cream?" he asked.

"Sure."

He frowned, as if still trying to figure out what she hid beneath her forced smile. Then, with a nod, he left and shut the door.

She eyed her phone, took a breath and texted, Where and when?

This was the best course of action to protect the family, the people she'd grown fond of in a way she hadn't thought possible.

She'd protect Jacob, make sure he didn't get hurt, wasn't separated from his daughter. Permanently.

Her phone dinged. 8 a.m. tomorrow. Grace's Diner.

Worried that the jerk might not keep his word and go after Miri anyway, Brie called Detective Harper. She informed him about the text messages and her plan to meet the stranger.

"You sure you want to take that risk?" he said. "What does the family think?"

"I don't want to involve them," Brie said. "Rose took Miri to her place, and I'm worried about them."

"I've got that covered. What time is the meet tomorrow? I'll send a few deputies."

"I don't want to scare him off."

"I'll send nonuniformed deputies. What time?"

"Eight. Grace's Diner."

Now she had to figure out a way to get there.

Brie had barely slept, planning her departure from the ranch without being noticed. She decided to ask Beau for a ride to the diner. He'd wanted her gone from day one, accusing her of bringing trouble to the ranch. It was easy to convince him to take her into town where she inferred she was meeting her research partner.

"Why didn't you ask Jacob for a ride?" Beau said.

"He would discourage me from leaving the premises." She glanced across the seat at Beau. "Whereas you want me gone."

"Nothing personal."

"I understand."

"When does your research partner arrive?"

"Soon."

"Maybe I should hang around."

"You don't want to miss church. I'll be fine."

"But you're gonna call Jacob and explain, right?"

"Sure." And she would, one day, once she was past all this danger and violence.

She owed Jacob that much. An explanation, an official thank-you for saving her life over and over again.

"Thank you for not saying anything to him."

"This suddenly feels wrong," Beau said.

"Think of it this way—you're protecting your family."

A family she'd be reluctant to leave behind.

Focus on the present situation. Brie had made a deal with her enemy to meet at the diner. She felt safe considering she'd be surrounded by other diners and plainclothes deputies.

Beau pulled into the parking lot.

"Thanks again." She opened the door.

"I feel like I should apologize," he said.

"For what? Wanting to protect your family? Not necessary. Take care, Beau."

She hopped out of the truck and entered the diner. Only four of the twelve or so tables were occupied. She chose the one closest to the window and spotted Beau's truck still parked in the lot. Why didn't he leave? She didn't want her pursuer to be scared off by Beau or the deputies. She scanned the restaurant, wondering if the deputies were any of the patrons in the restaurant. Two men, in their midthirties, were seated in a back booth drinking coffee. She assumed they were the officers Detective Harper had sent.

Draw him out, face your enemy and set him up to be arrested. That had been her grand plan. It seemed like her only choice if she wanted to protect her friends at the Boulder Creek Ranch.

It was nearly eight thirty when her phone dinged with a text: Buy a ticket for the Granite Falls tour.

She asked her server where she could get tour tickets, and she directed Brie to the drugstore across the street. Brie headed over there, figuring the deputies would follow her and the tour bus.

She got cash from the ATM in the drugstore and approached the counter to buy a bus ticket.

"How do you like working at the ranch?" the woman behind the counter asked.

Brie must have looked confused.

"We met the other day at the supply store? I'm Deidre, remember?"

"Oh, right, sorry. Yes, I enjoy the ranch very much," Brie answered.

With a quizzical frown, the woman handed Brie her ticket.

"Thanks." She took her ticket and went outside to board the bus. She noticed the two men from the diner, who she assumed were deputies, hovering on the sidewalk.

They were keeping a safe distance but would follow her.

She'd be okay.

A little over an hour later, they pulled into the Granite Falls lookout parking lot. There were only five people on the bus: a husband, wife and little boy and a teenage couple who were obviously in love. She stepped off the bus and took in the majestic beauty before her. For half a second she felt at peace, wishing she didn't have to leave this beautiful place.

"Snap out of it," she scolded. She needed to stay focused and alert.

She checked her phone.

A text instructed her to take the Tinder Trail north. She eyed the parking lot but didn't see the men from the diner, who she'd thought would follow her. She'd wait until they arrived before complying with her stalker's instructions.

Brie turned back to the panoramic view and took a deep breath. She'd learned so much about herself over the course of the past few days. She'd grown to believe in herself like she never had before.

To have faith. Thanks to Jacob.

"Such a beautiful view," a man said.

"Yes, it is." She turned.

And was looking at Stan's wicked smile.

A shudder ran down her spine.

"Everyone's enjoying it." He nodded toward the young family and the teenage couple, who held hands. "Wouldn't it be a shame if it's the last thing they ever see?" He opened his jacket to reveal a gun.

She peered around him.

"They're not coming. It's just you and me. Now, let's finish our hike."

THIRTEEN

Jacob pushed the speed limit as much as he could without getting pulled over.

Brianna had left to fight this battle on her own. Even after everything they'd been through together. Jacob thought she had come around, saw the value in letting other people help her through a crisis.

His phone rang, and he hit the speaker button.

"You find her?" Beau said.

"I'm not there yet." He tried keeping the edge out of his voice but was failing. Why did Beau dump her in town?

"Look, I'm sorry. I figured she was safe at the diner. Her lab partner was on the way, and I had to get back. I talked to Detective Harper. I guess she called him last night and filled him in on her plan."

"What plan? Throw herself into moving traffic? Because that's what it looks like from where

I'm sitting. No backup, no way to defend herself."

"Hang on, Harper sent plainclothes deputies to the diner."

"So, they're with her now?"

"No, they had car trouble and couldn't follow her."

"Car trouble? More like the guy figured out they were cops and messed with the car. This whole plan is nonsensical. What was she thinking?"

"She was trying to protect us—well, mostly you and Miri."

"I can't talk to you right now." Jacob clicked End. He felt like a jerk, but if he stayed on the phone with the guy who'd driven Brianna off ranch property, Jacob might say something even more rude.

"Lord, help me find her," he said softly.

He pulled into the diner lot and went inside. No Brianna.

The server remembered Brianna and said she'd asked about buying a tour bus ticket. A bus tour? But which one?

As Jacob dashed across the street to the drugstore, church bells rang in the distance. He'd miss church today, but he had good reason. The woman he was falling in love with was in danger.

There, he'd admitted it. He was falling in love with Dr. Brianna Wilkes.

He paused on the sidewalk. "God, help me out here. Don't let me lose her, too."

That's when it struck him that they'd shared locations through the phone app. He pressed the info button. The app was taking forever to load.

"Looking for your new wrangler?" He looked up as Deidre approached him. "The pretty blonde one?"

"You saw her?"

"Sure, I sold her a tour bus ticket a little while ago."

"To where?"

"I was covering for my daughter, who got in late from Boise last night. Thought I'd let her sleep, and Ernie didn't mind if I filled in so—"

He took her hands, and she stopped talking.

"Which bus? Where was it going?"

"Granite Falls."

"Thank you, thank you so much, Deidre."

Jacob sprinted back to his truck and called the detective. "Granite Falls. Brianna's gone to Granite Falls."

Brianna wasn't sure what was supposed to happen next. She and the creep named Stan were headed toward the falls. Why? Was he going to toss her over the edge?

After admitting he'd sabotaged the deputies' car and threatening to kill the tourists and driver of the bus if she called out for help, he'd persuaded Brie to surrender to her situation. He seemed to have the advantage, and she felt helpless.

Like when her sister died, her mother died and Dad abandoned her. She never wanted to feel that way again.

If the deputies were smart, they'd figure out what happened, that she'd bought a bus ticket to Granite Falls. She had to have faith they weren't far behind.

Faith. A new and powerful tool.

Somewhere in her bruised brain were cognitive skills that could get her out of this situation safely without involving others.

She tapped into those skills and decided to stall, buy time. Help was on the way. A plan formed in her mind.

"Where are we going, Stan?" she said.

"I thought fresh air might clear that head of yours. I need you to remember something."

He needed to bring her out here in this isolated part of the country so she could remember? And then what, make her disappear?

"So, how can I help?" she said, using Jacob's tactic with the armed teenager.

"Oh, now you want to help."

"Don't have much choice, do I?"

"I need to access your research."

"Why?"

"Why?" he countered.

"If you're going to steal my research and kill me, at least I should know why."

"I didn't say I was going to kill you."

"Well, you shot at the house last night—"

"To convince you to meet."

"You kidnapped me from Andrea's, and now you're threatening me at gunpoint. I deserve to know why."

"I needed to talk to you, but you kept gettin' away. Now I'll have your undivided attention."

She intentionally slipped and went down on her butt. "I obviously don't have the right shoes for this."

"Keep moving." He gripped her arm, pulling her to her feet.

Close, she was close enough to grab his gun—

He shoved her forward, and she stumbled. "I'm unsteady because I sprained my ankle that day you stalked me in the mountains."

"You're clumsy."

"No arguments there."

His expression softened. Was she making a connection?

"I'm glad you survived the car accident the other night," she said.

He shot her a look of disbelief.

"I don't want anyone to die."

She half hoped he'd agree with her, but he remained silent. They hiked another ten minutes in silence, and he didn't push her to pick up her pace. Maybe she was making a connection.

"We're almost there," he said.

Which meant she was running out of time to free herself, solve this mystery…

And to tell Jacob how she felt. She regretted that most of all.

They approached the end of the trail, an outlook with a steep drop to the falls below. No one would ever find her.

Would anyone even miss her? Before she'd come to Montana, probably not. But now? She'd like to think Jacob, the Rogers family, would.

Little Miri.

"I have only one question," he said. "If you answer it, you'll live."

She doubted it. She could describe him to authorities, which meant he'd always be a wanted man.

"I'll do my best," she said.

"I need the weekly access code to your research."

"I… I can't remember."

He backed her up against the protective metal railing meant to keep hikers safe. She peered over her shoulder at the steep drop. So much for buying time until help arrived.

"Please, if I knew I'd tell you."

"Do you want to die?" he ground out.

"Honest," she said. "It's the head injury."

"We both know you're lying." He pressed her into the metal railing. Only inches now, inches from falling to her death.

Oh, no. She wasn't done; she had more work to do, more people to help.

She jerked her knee into his crotch and grabbed his gun out of its holster. But before she could aim it, he grabbed her wrist and smacked it against the metal rail. The gun flew out of her hand.

"Password!" he shouted in her face. "Or I'll smash your head against the rail!"

"I… I can't remember!"

"I'll jar it loose for you."

Gripping her shoulders, he started to pull her toward him, gaining momentum to slam her against the railing.

"Password!"

She pinched her eyes shut. *God, please help me.*

Two gunshots rang out.

She gasped.

Stan released her, and she opened her eyes. With a surprised expression, he stumbled back a few steps and collapsed.

Behind him stood Jacob, clutching a gun with a trembling hand.

"Police! Hands where I can see 'em!" someone shouted.

Jacob, eyes locked on Stan's body, seemed frozen, unable to move.

Brianna fell to her knees. She was alive. Thanks to Jacob. Who couldn't even move, couldn't lower his arm or release the gun from his fingers.

Detective Harper came up beside him. "Jacob?"

Jacob didn't answer.

"You got him, buddy," Detective Harper said, gently lowering Jacob's arm. "We'll take it from here." He slipped the gun from Jacob's fingers and motioned to Brianna.

She went to Jacob and wrapped her arms around his waist. "You're here. I prayed for help, and He sent you." When Jacob didn't return the embrace, she placed her hand against his cheek and guided him to look at her.

The lost expression in his eyes took her breath away.

Later that day, Jacob stood in front of the main house at the Boulder Creek Ranch with the rest of the family and struggled to maintain his composure.

Brianna was leaving. For good.

Of course she was. She had a career in Chicago. He couldn't fault her for wanting to get back and finish her admirable research.

But a selfish part of him had prayed she would stay. Indefinitely.

At least she'd chosen to say goodbye to all of them in person this time.

When her lab partner met her at the police station, Jacob thought that might be the last time he would see her, that she'd drive away with Douglas. Perhaps it would have been better that way instead of like this, trying to mask his feelings that must be obvious to all.

He suspected he wouldn't heal from this heartbreak for a very long time.

Jacob took consolation in the fact she was no longer in danger. Although Detective Harper had turned the case over to the feds, he said they suspected that Stan had been hired by a drug company to access her research and sully her name, that the forged email exchange between Brianna and the drug company was meant to taint Brianna's reputation.

"I can't thank you enough for everything you've done for me," Brianna said to the group.

She didn't make eye contact with Jacob.

Miri hugged Brianna. "I don't want you to go."

Swallowing a ball of emotion, Jacob focused on the horses in the corral.

"I know, sweetie," Brianna said. "But I have to get back to work and let you all prepare for guests tomorrow."

"You'll come back next summer?"

"I'll try. It's been an honor to be a part of your family."

Jacob looked at her then, and she forced a smile. "I… I'll miss you," she said. "God bless."

She turned quickly, not giving Jacob a chance to respond, and rushed to the waiting SUV with her research partner behind the wheel. As they drove off, Miri called out her goodbyes and waved. The passenger window opened, and Brianna waved back.

"I hate when my friends leave," Miri said and stomped into the house.

"Yeah," Jacob said.

He noted looks of concern from his new family. "I've got work to do." He made for the barn. Hard labor, that's what he needed.

Rose and Beau followed, hovering close by. Jacob grabbed a pitchfork and went into a stall.

"What did she say, Rose?" Beau said.

"That she cares about him, a lot. I think she's in love with him."

"Then why'd she leave?"

Jacob glared at them. "Because she's got a life, a real life back in Chicago." He went back to his chore.

"She was afraid every time Jacob looked at her, he'd remember that day," Rose said. "The day he shot someone."

"Killed someone," Jacob corrected.

"In order to save her," Beau added.

"Brianna said she feared every time he'd look at her, he'd remember what she made him do—"

"She didn't make me do anything," Jacob muttered.

"And she cares about him too much to be a constant reminder of that trauma," Rose said.

"Leave me alone," Jacob said.

He thought they had, until Beau gave Jacob a shove from behind and he nearly went face-first into a pile of horse dung.

"Hey!" Jacob protested, turning around.

Rose shook her head and left the barn.

"Don't be an idiot," Beau said. "You love Brianna Wilkes."

Jacob glared at him. Was it that obvious?

"It doesn't matter how I feel."

"Oh, it matters," Beau countered. "Look, there isn't a day that goes by that I don't kick myself for not going after the woman I loved, for not telling her how I felt and asking her to stay."

"Why didn't you?" Jacob said.

"Pride? Ego? Fear of rejection? Take your pick. You'll never know if you don't try. And believe me, not knowing haunts you like nothing else."

"Briana's married to her work."

"So were you, once. All I'm saying is things change. Maybe the life-threatening experience of the past week has changed her view of life. I mean, she actually said 'God bless' when she left."

"Yeah, I noticed that, too."

"Jacob, if you had known about Cassie's pregnancy and where she'd gone, would you have come after her?"

"Absolutely."

"Then what's stopping you now?"

"It could never work. Brianna lives in Chicago. I live here."

"Empty excuses lead to an empty life. You have to try or else you'll always regret it. Trust me on that."

Jacob felt himself smile as he looked at Beau. "You should have been the therapist."

"With my patience?" Beau grabbed the pitchfork from Jacob. "I'll finish here. Go on, go talk to her."

Gazing out the window of the SUV, Brianna considered the immediate future spent clearing her name and getting her lab up and running.

The vast mountain range in the distance reminded her of what she was leaving behind. A week ago she'd come out West a city girl with no appreciation for the mountains or nature, yet now she was reluctant to leave, and not solely because of Montana's breathtaking beauty.

She regretted walking away from a kind and generous man and his adorable little girl.

Even though she'd said goodbye, something felt terribly wrong about leaving, about not seeing things through to the end.

What end? This was the end. At least of this particular chapter of her life and her chance at love.

"It was nice of Andrea to let us set up at the university for a few days," Douglas said.

"Yes, especially considering all she's been through because of me."

"I was surprised she offered to let you stay at her house. And that Rogers family, they're a bold group."

And protective, generous and caring.

Why was she leaving again? Oh, right. Her research. Which was temporarily on hold.

"Stan's connection to the drug company should go far in clearing my name," she said.

"Let's hope so."

"What I don't get is, I don't remember us being ready to publish, so why did the drug company feel suddenly threatened by our results?"

"Mind if we take the scenic route to the university?" Douglas said, turning onto a side road.

"You know where you're going?"

"I researched the area. It's gorgeous out here."

"Yes, it truly is." It filled her heart in a way she'd never experienced until she'd found her home in Montana.

Her home. Even throughout the tumultuous week of danger, she'd developed a sense of home here, specifically at the Boulder Creek Ranch with the Rogers family.

In that moment she knew that after she resolved things in Chicago, she'd come back west and start anew. Andrea had mentioned opportunities for Brianna at the university.

Then there was Jacob. Would he welcome her back? Did he feel the same way about Brianna?

"Don't look so worried," Douglas said. "Everything will be fine."

"Yes, it will be once I contact the drug companies tomorrow."

"For what purpose?"

"The emails inferred I spoke with someone intending to meet, but I don't remember that."

"The head injury."

"I don't think so."

Douglas took the next turn a little too fast.

"Careful, Douglas."

"Sorry."

They drove a few minutes in silence. When they ascended the mountain, she flashed back to when Stan had kidnapped her the other night, drove her up toward the lookout and nearly killed them both because he'd misjudged a turn.

"Maybe we should turn around," she said.

"I'll be more careful."

"It's just, I'm experiencing trauma from when that man kidnapped me and the car skidded off the road." She shuddered.

"Well, Stan's gone now. He can't hurt you anymore."

She snapped her attention to him. "I don't remember telling you his name." And she knew the police had kept details like that to themselves when questioning him.

"You must have," he said.

But she knew, without a doubt, that she hadn't.

He must have read her expression, because he jerked the car onto the shoulder.

"Let's take in the beautiful view," he said.

Brianna didn't move at first, struggling to make sense of it. The only way he could know Stan's name was if…

"I said out!" He pulled a Taser from beneath the seat and aimed it at her.

She opened her door and scrambled out of the truck.

"I don't understand," she said as he joined her by the side of the road. "Why would you do this?"

"Because you were never going to release our findings. 'We have to prove our thesis beyond question,'" he mimicked. "'We have to make sure there's no question about its integrity.' I spent five years of my life on a project that would establish my name in the research community, and you were holding us back!"

"Douglas, you know we have to challenge our own findings to prove they're accurate. You wouldn't want to report conclusions that—"

"We were ready! Why couldn't you see that?" he shouted, waving the Taser.

Brie kept backing up, trying to put distance between them so as not to give him a clear shot.

"Douglas, let's talk about this. You don't want to do anything you'll regret."

"Oh, I won't regret taking over the lab after you're gone."

Keep him talking, she thought. *Make a connection.* It hadn't worked with Stan, but this was different. She knew Douglas personally.

"I had no idea you were so frustrated," she said.

"Of course not. It was all about you, only you."

Had she been that self-focused? That oblivious?

"I'm sure we can figure something out," she said.

"You've left me no choice. I have commitments to keep."

Which meant he'd made deals with drug companies? Perhaps taken money from powerful people?

"But, Douglas, we're a team," she tried.

"We were never a team! It was always about you, the lead researcher, the brilliant woman who came from nothing."

"How about we—"

"I'll tell authorities we discovered more evidence proving you made drug companies jockey for position to buy our research, driving up the price. You blocked it out due to the head injury, but then when you started to remember, you grew despondent. You went for a hike to be alone with your thoughts, your guilt. And you never returned."

"No one will believe that."

"They will when I give them access to your online journal confessing your criminal plans, your guilt, your slide into depression."

"I don't have a journal."

He smiled. He'd obviously created the journal to support his story.

"Douglas, listen to me. I'm no threat to you anymore. I've decided I want something different, a different kind of life."

And she meant it.

"What, out here? You must really think I'm an idiot."

"Things have changed. I've changed."

"You've found God," he mocked.

It was partially true. She had opened her heart to God, but she had also fallen in love with a remarkable man.

"Keep walking!" Douglas shouted.

A car horn suddenly blared as a vehicle sped toward them. Taking advantage of the distraction, Brie charged Douglas, knocking the Taser from his hand and shoving him away. He stumbled, lost his balance and fell over the edge of the road into the ravine.

She scrambled to see into the steep drop below but couldn't make out Douglas's figure.

A car door slammed behind her, drawing her attention. She looked up to see Jacob approach.

"Jacob? What are you...? How did you find me?" she said.

He pulled out his phone. "Location-sharing app. Didn't think you'd mind."

She threw her arms around his neck and held on tight.

"Guess I was right."

"Help! Somebody help!" Douglas's voice echoed.

"We'd better call Emergency," Jacob said.

She sighed and looked up at him. "You always find me, don't you?"

"I guess that's because—" he smiled "—I love you."

She hugged him and never wanted to let go.

Six months later

The Rogers family, gathered around the dinner table, had just finished saying their prayer of thanks when a car door slammed outside.

"She's here! She's here!" Miri shouted, rushing to the window.

Jacob stood, his gut a tangle of anticipation, as it was most times Brianna was near. He was a sap in love, that's for sure.

"Do you have something to share, Jacob?" Lacey said.

They were all looking at him, wearing knowing smiles.

"Sorry, no." He sat down.

"Just go answer the door already," Beau muttered, squirting ketchup on his burger.

"I got it!" Miri flung the door open and hugged Brianna's leg. "We thought you got stuck in the snow."

Jacob approached as she entered the great room, Detective Harper behind her.

"I could have picked you up," Jacob said, kissing her cheek.

"I had to come out this way, so I offered Brianna a ride," the detective said, glancing across the room at Rose.

"Join us for dinner, T.J.," Lacey said.

"Yeah, join us," Rose said.

Beau snorted.

"What?" Rose challenged.

"Nothin'."

"You're a jerk," Rose said.

"Takes one to—"

"Would you stop?" Lacey said. "T.J., come sit

by me. Jacob, take Brianna's coat. We want to hear all the news."

Jacob hung Brianna's coat on the rack by the door.

"It's good news on my end." T.J. sat next to Rose. "The feds have a solid case against Brianna's lab partner, so she's been completely cleared."

"And research results will be published next week," Brianna offered.

"So, it's ready?" Jacob said.

"It is. With help from Mr. Jenson, I was able to finish the project to my satisfaction. We were so close. If only Douglas would have been patient."

Jacob squeezed her hand. "You'll be a superstar."

"As long as the protocols help people...that's all that matters," she said.

Jacob led her to the table.

"I suppose you'll have to travel the world for speaking engagements?" Lacey said.

"For a few months."

"And then?" Jacob sat next to her, their legs touching.

"The university has asked me to join their staff, both to teach a class on research and... wait for it."

The Rogers clan stopped eating, and everyone looked at her.

"They want me to open a lab at the university to broaden my research to cover children."

"That's fantastic," Lacey said.

"Sounds like a lot of work," Rose said.

"It's not work if you love what you do, is it?" She looked at Jacob.

"No, ma'am, it's not."

"Besides, I'll always make time for what's important." She shared a smile with the group and then pinned Jacob with her soft brown eyes.

He'd never, in his life, thought he'd find this kind of connection again.

He'd never thought he'd fall in love.

"Go on, kiss her," Beau said, placing his hand over Miri's eyes.

"Ew, no kissing at the table," Miri protested.

"Kiss her, kiss her!" they sang.

And when he did, he felt whole, like he never had before. He thanked God for bringing this woman into his life and giving them the chance to live a bright and hopeful future, blessed with love and family.

* * * * *

Look for more books in
Hope White's Boulder Creek Ranch series,
coming soon from Love Inspired Suspense!

Get 4 FREE REWARDS!

We'll send you 2 FREE Books plus 2 FREE Mystery Gifts.

Harlequin Heartwarming Larger-Print books will connect you to uplifting stories where the bonds of friendship, family and community unite.

FREE Value Over $20